MURDER AND MACARONI

A Cannoli Cafe Cozy Mystery

LIZZIE BENTON

http://lizziebenton.com

For my Family

AUTHOR'S NOTE

In my personal experience as a life-long resident of New Jersey, most people refer to the plural form of "cannoli" as "cannolis" in conversation. Therefore, the dialogue in this book reflects that.

While the origin of "cannoli" traces back to the singular form "cannolo," I've never actually heard anyone use that word, even in my local Italian bakeries! (Most people will ask for "a cannoli" or they will specify a number of "cannolis" they want to order.) Perhaps other areas or bakeries could be different, but I've written this fictional series to reflect some of the local Italian-American flavor I personally encountered growing up.

PROLOGUE

Nicole Capula strained to see as the whole room began to fade. Blackness crept into her vision, until it completely enveloped her. Paralyzed, she lost her balance and her strength.

Fortunately, someone caught her before her head hit the floor.

CHAPTER ONE

"Professor, I want my macaroni!" shouted Mr. Don Martini. The Knights chess club was holding its typical Tuesday night get-together at the Cannoli Cafe.

"At least you're addressing her properly now," remarked Max, his opponent for the evening once again. Don grunted and resumed staring at his chess board.

Nicole approached their table, bearing a tray with two small bowls of Italian baked macaroni. Eyeing the board, she noticed that Don was about to lose. "Good evening, gentlemen. Why does this feel like deja vu, or does it?" she asked with a twinkle in her eye. As she placed the bowls on the table along with the parmesan cheese shakers, she suddenly felt a chill go down her spine. She shuddered as she recalled the chain of events that followed the last time she served the old men at her cafe. *At least there won't be a heart attack or a murder this time,* she thought.

Max gave Nicole a friendly wink. "See Don, I told you she's brilliant. How many people get a Ph.D. in chemical engineering? A fraction of a fraction of one-percent of the population, in fact. She's a smart lady —she knows you're about to lose! Checkmate!"

Nicole shook her head and chuckled. "You're very kind. Please let me know if you need anything else," she said with a warm smile.

Max returned Nicole's smile and said, "Let's have cannolis, in about twenty minutes!" He nodded his head up and down very excitedly, reminding Nicole of her black labrador, Ringo, when he wanted one of his treats. Meanwhile, a red-faced Mr. Martini started talking to himself as he analyzed his position on the board.

"Of course! Enjoy your macaroni!" said Nicole. She realized they probably didn't hear her reply since they started arguing again, as usual. She left the tray on a stand near the entrance to the kitchen and eyed her best friend, Lia, who was sitting on a stool at the front counter. Lia appeared to be furiously engaged in something she was viewing on her laptop. "Is everything okay, Lia?"

"Yes, I'm just a bit stressed. A new client hired me

after tax day to sort out a huge mess. On top of that, it doesn't look like he provided the latest forms summarizing capital gains and dividends from the financial institutions. They tend to issue correction after correction, instead of sending them right the first time." Lia barely looked up from her computer as she spoke to her best friend.

Nicole remembered her friend mentioning something about that a few months earlier, around the time they had solved the murder mystery concerning the library director.

"I know I've been running my accounting practice a couple of years now. I should be used to these tough situations, but this particular one is stressing me out." Lia rubbed her eyes and sighed.

"I know what will cheer you up!" Nicole took out a few macaroon cookies from the front case and arranged them on a plate. Then she added a fresh cannoli to the dish and drizzled her signature chocolate sauce on the hard, flaky crust before handing the plate over to her friend. Lia finally looked up, eager to accept her dessert, just as Nicole suddenly experienced another wave of unease pass through her body.

Not wasting any time, Lia took a bite out of a macaroon cookie. "Mmm. These cookies are unbelievable. As I've said before, I can't get enough of this almond taste. You should stop teaching part-time at the university and look into selling these as a product in stores instead. That would really put your cafe on the map!"

Nicole shook her head. "You know I love teaching part-time. It keeps me current and stimulates my mind a bit, without too much pressure. Plus the college kids help me feel...young." Nicole stared down at her feet, arms crossed.

"Please, you're only turning thirty-six this summer! It's all in your head. You need to stop *acting* old!" Lia closed her laptop, finally laughing a bit. "In all seriousness, though, you've been seeming a bit...I don't know, melancholy?" Lia said.

Nicole's eyes widened, but she kept her eyes on the floor. "I'm okay," she said, slightly stammering.

"Are you *really* okay? You're not your usual self, Nicole. What is it—the aging thing, or no kids yet thing, or problems in the Dean department?" Lia chewed on her lip, appearing slightly concerned, before she picked up the second cookie off her plate.

Lia's questions threw Nicole off slightly. She raised her head to meet Lia's line of sight. "Dean and I are taking it slowly. With his private investigator business, along with my teaching and running the cafe, it's been hard to squeeze in a few dates here and there. And I think we're both treading carefully given our history." She paused and then added, with slightly upturned lips, "But I am *truly* enjoying his company. He's unlike many of the men I used to work with in the chemical industry. He's got this unique combination of being strong mentally and physically, but he can also be tender-hearted. He was always like that, I suppose, even all the way back in high school, but I think he has matured quite a bit, especially since, you know—" Appearing flushed, she looked down again. Her brow furrowed as she noticed a spot on the mostly sparkling counter. She grabbed a clean rag and wiped the blemish, revealing a shiny surface once again.

"So what are you not telling me? What's wrong? I know something is up with you. Can I have a cappuccino, by the way? I'm going to be up late tonight and need the caffeine." Lia started putting her laptop away in her oversized fashion bag.

"Of course," said Nicole. She took a moment to prepare the cappuccino. After frothing the milk, she said, "Well, I know the police department gave me that civilian award for solving the murder of the library director, Frank Tanner, a few months ago. But, the truth is, I don't feel very worthy." Nicole shook cinnamon over the cup and slid Lia's cappuccino in her direction. She then sat down opposite her friend. "I've just been feeling bad about it. Someone died in Aunt Lucia's restaurant, and as we were attempting to piece together what happened, I just got lucky. I didn't really do anything novel like those famous detectives do."

"Thank you for this, once again," Lia's eyes softened as she gestured to her cappuccino. "Nicole, you're my dear friend, and you know I'm always direct. The thing is, everyone *loves* you. Why do you think the whole town talks to you? Your genuine nature draws them in. Look at how Bernadette bequeathed you this very cafe, and then you were in the cafe when you heard a critical piece of information. You figured out what needed to be done before there was another victim. If you didn't love helping people, whether it was through your teaching or running this place, you might not have saved her in time." Nicole noticed Lia was looking directly into her eyes, as if she was trying to gently burn the sentiment into her.

Nicole's eyes moistened. "You and Dean played a big part in all that, too. Well...thanks, I needed that reassurance." Nicole took a tissue from her pocket and dabbed her eyes. "I'm just trying to adjust to all these changes, you know. Giving up my career in the chemical industry, becoming the new owner of the Cannoli Cafe, dating Dean, moving back to Rosewood. It's been a lot. Plus, we had the added concern about Aunt Lucia's health when the murder happened in her restaurant."

"Don't be so hard on yourself. You have experienced *major* changes quite recently. How is Aunt Lucia, by the way?" asked Lia.

Nicole's mouth formed a big smile at the mention of her aunt. "She is doing well, thank goodness. She did great at her last check-up. And she is following the doctor's orders and resting. She is down in Little Egg Harbor right now while Dan Morano is managing her trattoria in her absence."

"That's great! Who can complain about the smell of the ocean and being on the relaxing lagoon in the summertime. And at least she's in driving distance." Lia finished all her cookies and was eyeing her cannoli, eager to dive in.

"That's the great thing about New Jersey, right? We can go to New York City or the shore on a whim!" Nicole brightened. "Thanks, I'm feeling a little better now. You helped me gain perspective. I can always count on you for that!"

Nicole's spirits had indeed lifted a bit after hearing her friend's words. She was reminded of everything she was grateful for during the conversation—from living in New Jersey to having special friends and family members. She would have felt even better, though, if she could shake an inexplicable feeling of trepidation that just wouldn't go away.

"True. And now for my *favorite*," announced Lia. Just as she lifted the cannoli to her lips, the front door burst open. It was the police chief, Commissioner Melvin Van Stone. "Stop, don't eat that cannoli! Everyone, don't move, don't eat, don't do anything!"

Suddenly, a number of police officers and detectives were inside the Cannoli Cafe. Nicole, stunned, watched them place yellow caution tape across her front windows and door. Meanwhile, patrons looked very confused. Max and Don stopped arguing. Their eyes darted around the room as they took in the scene unfolding before them.

Dean ran inside, ducking under the tape. Nicole searched his eyes, confused. Before he could say anything, the police commissioner said, "Nicole, I need to bring you to the police station. That reporter for the Rosewood Gazette, Stuart Helm, died tonight eating one of your cannolis."

CHAPTER TWO

One week prior to the murder

"I'm sorry, Dad," Gregory said, his lips quivering. He was shaking all over and could not seem to keep his body steady as he sat across the desk from his father.

"Not only did you cheat, but you got caught! And that ridiculous Stuart Helm wrote all about it, and now it's plastered in the newspapers and all over the internet. What were you thinking?" asked Rosewood business administrator, Mr. Thomas Gornick. They were sitting in his office at the town hall, across the street from Rosewood Park.

Knock, knock, knock.

"Don't move, we're not through," said Mr.

Gornick to his son. The door opened slightly. It was Mayor Diane Eckel.

She stepped inside. "Hi, Tom. Hello, Gregory. Listen, I know this is a bad time. I just saw...well, you know. I wanted to let you know I won't be expecting that revised budget analysis this week. Feel free to take a few days off for your family."

"Thanks, Diane. I appreciate it. I think I will need a few days after all," answered Tom, gritting his teeth.

Just as the mayor was about to exit, she turned back and said, "I know most colleges will revoke Gregory's acceptance now, but perhaps we can talk with Nicole and have her put in a word at the University of New Jersey."

"Nicole who? You're not talking about the owner of the Cannoli Cafe, are you? Why would we need *her* help?" Tom asked.

"Because she has a good relationship with the university. They wanted her to serve in the administration actually, but she prefers to teach there on a minimal basis instead. Apparently she's more interested in her freedom and running a business, and she's doing a great job of it, I must say. Anyway, maybe she can convince them to enroll Gregory and give him a chance."

"He didn't even apply there. It's beneath us, in fact," responded Tom.

"Tom, their graduates compete with alumni from top schools around the country in business and engineering positions. Can't be that bad. Besides, *I* graduated from there," said the mayor. She raised an eyebrow at Tom and walked out.

Fuming, Tom Gornick rose from his leather chair and closed his office door. Now facing the window, he noticed the sunset streaking on the surface of the lake across the street.

"You're grounded for eternity. Why did you do this, Gregory?"

Gregory did not dare turn his head to look at his father. Instead, he also stared straight ahead, his eyes fixed on the fountain spewing water in the middle of the lake. Suddenly, he felt his father's hands firmly grip his shoulders.

"I, uh, I...you said I needed to get into your alma mater. There was no way I could get straight A's earlier this year. I'm sorry, Dad. I regret it, but I was desperate. I'm not as smart as the other kids in the class! And I only did it for that one exam!" Gregory began to sob.

"Get a grip, Gregory. Stop crying. You're about to turn eighteen." Tom Gornick walked around his office, pacing.

"I'm sorry!" Gregory grabbed some tissues out of the box on his father's desk.

"I can't totally blame you. Kids have low points and succumb to the pressure sometimes. But the one time you did, that Stuart Helm caught you." Tom asked, practically screaming, "How did that happen?"

"He had interviewed me about some of my teachers earlier this year. And then he was lurking around the school a lot, looking for stories, I think. I don't know...I've been wracking my brain, trying to figure out how this happened." Gregory paused while he tried to compose himself. "Come to think of it, I think he swiped some papers from my backpack. He had asked me to step out of a classroom to get a particular book from my locker during an interview. He wanted to know more about one of the teachers who wrote their own textbook. I noticed the papers were missing when I got home that night."

"You have to be kidding me. What kind of person is this guy, stealing from a kid?" Thomas Gornick made it back to his desk and slammed his right fist down.

"Dad, could he have targeted me because of your resentment towards his family? Maybe he was trying to get to you?" Gregory asked, a bit nervously. "It worked," he said sheepishly.

Tom slammed both hands on his desk, his jaw

squared off. "Doesn't matter now. I will have the last word, believe me." Tom paused. Rubbing his hands together, he said, "He ruined your chances of going to any of the top schools. He is going to pay!"

Gregory watched his father in disbelief. He knew better than to question him and really didn't want to know what his father had in mind. He was mostly worried about what to do about college now that he was in such a mess.

Thomas tapped his forehead, thinking. "I am going to get him, and I will get him good. And maybe I'll get that stupid local hero, Nicole, while I'm at it. She needs to be knocked down a bit. She thinks she's so smart with her three degrees and all. These people from low-level schools aren't truly successful. The town will see that very soon."

CHAPTER THREE

"Nicole! Nicole! Wake up!" shouted Dean. "Susie, can you get some water?"

"Now, watch what you serve her. This cafe could be contaminated!" said the police commissioner, Melvin Van Stone.

"I have a brand new bottle right here," answered Susie. She was wide-eyed as she watched the scene before her. Dean was low to the ground, holding Nicole in his arms, appearing desperate to wake her up.

Nicole started to open her eyes. "Dean?"

"Here you go. Drink this," he said, with a sigh of relief.

"What happened?" Nicole asked.

"Oh, dear, you've had quite a shock. We think you simply fainted when you heard the news," said Susie.

Suddenly, it all came back to Nicole. Still in Dean's arms, she shifted her eyes around the cafe. She observed caution tape, officers, and no patrons. Lia was still on the front stool, and the commissioner and Susie were looking down at them.

"Commissioner Van Stone, what did you say about Stuart Helm?" asked Nicole. She was still half on the floor. Dean started to help her up to a chair.

"I'm sorry, maybe I was a bit rash, Nicole. I know you were a big help to the department in the last murder case. Maybe we can do the questioning right here," said the commissioner.

"'I'm confused. Did you say he died eating one of my cannolis?" Nicole looked over at Susie, who had been in the kitchen all night warming the meals for the Knights.

"Yes, well that is how it appears. There was a Cannoli Cafe box on his desk with a half-eaten cannoli in his hand when we responded to the call. Danielle Pruitt, a fellow reporter, had walked into the office this evening and noticed he was slumped over in his chair, with his head on his desk. First, she simply thought he was sleeping. But when he didn't get up for a while, she went over to him and realized something wasn't right. She called 9-1-1 at that point."

Dean piped up. "Nicole, what's wrong?"

"I just feel very dizzy. It's just so shocking. What

can I do to help? There's no way he died from my cannolis, and now I need to prove it," answered Nicole.

The commissioner looked at Dean and then Nicole. "Actually, we're giving Detective Dwight Dawkins a second chance to solve a murder. You did his job last time, if you know what I mean. He's in the back now working with a team to collect samples of all of your ingredients."

"But I have a very strict system! If you tell me the number on the box, I can tell you which batch the cannolis are from, and then direct you to the exact containers of ingredients I had used and even when they were purchased," said Nicole, worried.

"She's right. Bernadette was not as rigorous. Honestly, it was stressful learning Nicole's approach at first. She adapted her laboratory and plant best practices to the cafe, believe it or not. She is constantly talking about traceability," said Susie.

Commissioner Van Stone raised his eyebrows and then looked at Nicole. "Really?" he asked.

"I didn't look at the cafe batches of food or baked goods any differently than I looked at batches of chemical product when I first arrived." Nicole took another sip of water and sat more upright in her chair, feeling a little stronger. "For instance, I hate when I visit a restaurant or cafe and the food tastes different from one time to the next. My system helps prevent that from happening. Around the time I first took over the cafe, we had received a bad shipment of pumpkin pie spice. We had terrible-tasting pumpkin pie as a result. This was around Thanksgiving. Because of the traceability, I could identify the exact lot number of the pumpkin spice used. I then contacted the pumpkin spice supplier. They later confirmed they had made a mistake and thanked us for our insight!"

Susie offered, "I can go to the back and show the detective where we record the information about each batch. Did you say you know the number of the batch from the box?"

"No, but we have the box in evidence so we should be able to figure that out. We're also testing the half-eaten cannoli for toxicity. For now, maybe we can determine when Stuart Helm bought the cannolis and start there? Do either of you remember?" asked Commissioner Van Stone.

Nicole said, "I don't recall him being here in the last few days. In fact, he hasn't been here in over a month."

Susie nodded. "I haven't seen him either. Typically it's one of us ringing up customers at the front if they stop in for baked goods."

Dean looked at the commissioner and said, "So

someone must have given him cannolis. We should confirm who has been here the last forty-eight hours along with the number on the box. Nicole, what about your video surveillance?"

"I have a program on my computer in the back. It has all the video footage."

Detective Dwight Dawkins suddenly appeared in the doorway of the kitchen. He said in a raised voice, "I got your computer. I'm taking it to the station."

"Okay, but please don't erase anything. I have everything from my course notes to—" Nicole's voice trailed off.

Dean gave Nicole a quizzical look. "To what, Nicole?"

"My n-n-novel," she answered.

Lia, who had been silent the whole time, still on the front stool, spoke up, "Oh, dear! Can someone please just tell me if I can eat my cannoli?"

CHAPTER FOUR

One week prior to the murder

Danielle Pruitt sat across the desk from her editor. She tapped her foot lightly on the floor, trying to hide her exasperation. "But June, Stuart gets all the major stories. He got the exclusive on Nicole Capula confronting Frank Tanner's murderer! When am I going to get something like that? I've been here much longer than him! What happened to seniority?"

"Danielle, Stuart found this particular juicy topic all on his own. I can't give it away. You need to earn it!" June lowered her head as she looked back at Danielle, her hazel eyes just clearing her dark horn-rimmed glasses.

"But I can't earn it if you continue to assign me to

cover events such as basketball games, parades and mundane things like that. If I'm always out on assignment, I can't be in the right time and place, so-to-speak, to grab the exclusives. Is there any chance you can cut me a break and let me find something newsworthy?" Danielle was not only tapping her foot at this point, but rubbing her hands together under the edge of June's desk.

"Let me tell you something. This story about the business administrator's son is going to help us sell papers and advertising for our online platform. It's very hard to stay in business these days, and the owner appreciates that Stuart is single-handedly contributing to our bottom line, something you haven't figured out how to do yet!"

"I would love to contribute to the bottom line, if you would only gave me a chance!" Danielle pleaded with her editor. June shook her head and started paging through the latest revision on the newspaper.

Danielle waited for a response from June, but after she got none, she jumped up from her chair so quickly that June finally flinched. "Okay, June. I'm heading to the game now." She walked out of June Trainor's office and headed straight for the office water cooler. After swallowing two full cups, her friend, Dina, approached her.

"Everything okay, Danielle?" Dina asked, her voice shaking just a touch.

"No. I don't know how I'm going to ever move up around here. Everything is Stuart-Stuart-Stuart! It's ridiculous." She sighed before pushing the handle down one last time to get a third cup of water. "Follow me." The webmaster complied and stayed close to Danielle while they made their way to her desk in the open area. No one was around, besides June in her office, since it was evening. The other reporters didn't have to cover stories like sports games or non-major events.

After lowering herself into the uneven chair across from Danielle, Dina said, "Is there anything I can do?"

"I might ask you to teach me how to code, because I'm not seeing much opportunity here going forward." Danielle said, sarcastically.

"I'd love to teach you. Actually I was putting together an online course. Maybe I can show you some of my videos and you can learn—" Before Dina could finish, Danielle interrupted her.

"I'm so angry. I hate June and this place. I don't get why they love Stuart so much. He's just so arrogant. I bet I could find better exclusives in this sleepy old town if I had the chance. I just need him to get out of my way."

"How would he get out of the way, June? Maybe you can fill in for him if he goes on vacation and then they'll see what a great reporter you are?" Dina asked.

"He never goes on vacation because he doesn't like missing opportunities." She paused while she looked up at the ceiling, appearing to be in thought. "No, I have a better idea. A permanent one, in fact," Danielle said. The sparkle of her teeth peeked out from her lips as she released a slight smile.

"I don't know what you mean," said Dina, mystified.

"Don't worry about it. I have it all figured out," she said, sitting more upright than she had earlier. "Hey, let's go get cannolis from that cafe. I want to indulge before spending my evening with a bunch of sweaty high schoolers. Besides, I need to do a little bit of *research*."

CHAPTER FIVE

Dean crept up the driveway with his SUV.

"What about my car? I left it at the cafe," Nicole asked, worried about leaving it there overnight.

"I'll take care of it with one of my buddies, if you give me your keys. You'll see your car right here in this spot, in place of mine, when you wake up tomorrow!"

"If you think that's best—" started Nicole. "I feel so embarrassed about passing out." She handed her keys over to Dean, grateful he was there to help her.

Before she could continue, Dean said, "You're being too hard on yourself. Of course it's shocking to hear someone died from eating one of your cannolis."

Nicole's eyes widened once again. This time, however, she felt more angry than weak. "I am going to get to the bottom of this. This reminds me of my years in the chemical industry. I thought I could let my guard down here, but it seems like someone is always out to get to me." Tears formed in the corners of her eyes.

Nicole took her seat belt off and started to unlock the door. Before she got out, she said, "People love to play games. It's sort of a survival thing. I don't know if it's because they feel threatened around me or what, but I've had my share of people attempting to make me look bad or discredit me behind my back. Those incidents really shook me—" she said, her voice trailing off.

"And I'm sure those situations made you a lot stronger, too. I must admit, I noticed the naivete you had about the world back in high school seems to be a distant memory now. You used to have so much faith in people." Dean hesitated. "You still do with some individuals, but I can tell you've changed your expectations a great deal. I just hope you might have a little faith in those who care about you. You know, Lia...and me. "

Dean's comment surprised Nicole. She realized he turned out to be quite perceptive. He, too, was a bit naive about the world years ago, perhaps why they gelled so well in high school. Nicole remembered that he just "wanted to catch the bad guys" to make the world a better place when he talked about his future career. She thought about how when you're young, it's hard to understand the evil that drives people, or even how every person in life bears their own set of wounds and experiences, shaping their behavior. One may think: "This person is good, " or "Here's a bad apple," but in reality, there are shades of gray everywhere.

Realizing she got lost in thought, Nicole shifted her eyes to meet Dean's gaze. He responded, "Shall we? I'll help you get settled and then I'll leave you with Lia." They both exited the car and proceeded up her walk.

Nicole laughed when she saw a familiar face by her front door—with a suitcase. "Lia! I should have known you'd take advantage of the opportunity to sleep over again. I think you like eating out of my refrigerator and watching my television!" Nicole felt a touch lighter after all that heavy thinking and smiled.

"Can't deny it! How are you feeling?" she asked.

Nicole eyed Lia's rolling suitcase again and took in her happy disposition. "Better now. I'm ready to solve this murder, with my good friends!"

"That's right. And someone has to take care of you, that's why I'm here!" Lia said. Dean opened the front door while Lia took Nicole in one arm and rolled her suitcase with the other. Once they were inside the living room, Lia said, "I'm going to go put this around the corner myself. I'll make us some tea in a minute." Spotting Nicole's dog, she added, "Hi, Ringo!"

Ringo, Nicole's black labrador retriever, revealed his friendly bark. Nicole stroked his fur and greeted him. Seeming satisfied, he went back to his doggie bed in the corner of the living room, clearly more interested in gnawing on one of this toys.

Dean and Nicole sat down on the sofa next to each other. Lia returned quickly and put the kettle on in the kitchen.

"Can't I help you?" Nicole raised her voice so that Lia could hear her.

"No, just sit there with your boyfriend." Lia proceeded to take three mugs out of the cabinet and also opened the refrigerator door to retrieve the milk.

Boyfriend, Nicole thought. She knew she was dating Dean, but hadn't quite looked at him as a "boyfriend." Since she was mid 30s, she wondered if there should be a more mature term for him, if he was in fact "steady" with her. *Gentleman-friend?* She wondered.

"Speaking of which," Dean said, stunning Nicole. "I made reservations for Saturday night at Chez Juliette at the shore. I will pick you up at 5."

"Oh?" Nicole asked. Her back was to Lia in the

kitchen, but she knew Lia had to be listening to their conversation.

"I have really enjoyed seeing you these past few months, but honestly I feel like the whole town is watching us all the time. I thought it would be nice to go an hour out and see the ocean, enjoy fine dining and have a chance to spend time together, just the two of us. You know, without the whole town coming along." Dean rubbed his forehead momentarily.

"But what if we haven't solved the murder by then? I'm not going to be great company if my cafe is closed. I'm hoping I can re-open it in the next day or so," Nicole said in a worried tone.

"I have faith that you'll figure it out." He took her hand in his.

"Why don't you try and stop me? It might be dangerous. You're the private investigator, after all."

"I know better than to get in your way. And I figure we make a good team this way. Gives me an excuse to call you and call on you a bit more." He winked. "Just make sure you stick to research. No confrontations this time!"

Lia appeared from the kitchen doorway with a tray. She had three mugs with a ginger tea bag in each. "I remember how effective the ginger tea was during our last investigation." She handed a mug and napkin to Nicole and Dean, and then set a mug down on the coffee table for herself. "Let me return this tray to the kitchen. When I get back, I'll have my legal pad and we can finally start brainstorming!"

Once Lia sat down, with several different colored pens in hand, Dean spoke up, "What do we know about Stuart Helm?"

"He's a reporter for the Rosewood Gazette," offered Lia.

Nicole took a sip from her mug. "Stuart wrote the article about how we solved the murder of Frank Tanner, and he emphasized my role in it versus Detective Dawkins. Here, I have it saved on the lower shelf of my coffee table." She brought it out and started leafing through the paper.

"Danielle Pruitt is a reporter at the paper—" Dean said, his voice trailing off.

"Yes, Dean? Something you want to share?" Lia asked, in a funny tone.

"Well, she has expressed a bit of interest in me, as of late. I can't figure out if it's genuine or if she simply wants inside information for a future article." Nicole's eyes widened as she listened. For the first time in a while, she felt a slight pang of jealousy. She glanced at Lia who gave her the slightest look before pursuing the conversation further with Dean.

"Why are you bringing it up? Do you think she has something to do with the murder?" asked Lia. She held her mug in both hands, leaning forward in her chair, a few feet from Nicole's fireplace.

"I think we should look into her, yes. She was pretty assertive with me when I first returned to town, and particularly when Frank Tanner was murdered."

"What?" Nicole piped up.

"Well, you and I were just getting reacquainted back then, and I didn't feel it was worth bringing up. But Danielle called me quite a bit and kept stopping by my office that week, hoping to get the inside scoop. She also flirted with me. But I told her I was interested in someone else."

"Aha! So, Danielle could have launched a two-prong attack...kill her competition at the Gazette, Stuart Helm, and frame Dean's love interest, Nicole, in the process! Plus Nicole did play a big part in the last murder mystery!" Lia said enthusiastically. Nicole and Dean both stared at Lia in response. "What? I love this stuff! Not sure why I took up accounting!"

Nicole, feeling nervous and shaken, continued to rub her chin. "Well, she's our first suspect. Any other ideas?" Lia and Dean both shook their heads. Nicole noticed that Dean appeared uneasy and had turned pale.

"I think I will pay a visit to see the new library

director, Christina Morano, tomorrow," said Nicole suddenly.

"Really, why?" asked Lia.

"I want to see if she can help me search the newspaper archives. Maybe if we can see who or what Stuart wrote about the past year, we can pinpoint a few possible enemies he could have made."

"That's a good idea," Dean said in a low voice.

"What's the matter, Dean?" asked Nicole.

"I'm worried about who was really targeted in Stuart's murder. What if they weren't really targeting Stuart, but in fact trying to frame you, Nicole. Maybe they just wanted to poison him, not necessarily kill him. Or maybe they were trying to get him to write about food poisoning in your cafe or something. We don't know what they were aiming for. But they killed Stuart regardless so we have to be careful." He took her hand in his. Nicole felt a lump in her throat as she observed his furrowed eyebrows. She was taken back by his concern.

"Yes, someone who could be mad at Nicole. You know I heard the Rosewood Coffee Shoppe has been hurting for customers since Nicole took over the Cannoli Cafe." Lia stood up and started pacing across Nicole's living room.

Nicole, feeling sick to her stomach, said, "Bert Davison owns that cafe. He seems like a tough guy.

Maybe he's angry that my cafe is doing pretty well right now."

"True," said Dean. "Now I am a little more concerned." Dean squeezed Nicole's hand even harder.

"So what should we do?" asked Nicole.

"I'll see what I can find out from my sources. Don't worry about it for now." Dean stood up. "And I think you should go the library and pursue your research tomorrow." He was still holding Nicole's hand in his. "It's late and you should get some rest. I'll take Ringo out for a few minutes. I don't want you to go out in the dark alone from now on. I think you should start getting ready for the night. Go take a hot shower and relax. I'll bring Ringo back to Lia and make sure she locks up."

Before Nicole could object, he hugged her tightly and gave her a soft kiss on her lips before walking out the door with Ringo.

"He's so worried about you, Nicole," said Lia. "Well, I am too a little bit, now that we took a few minutes to analyze the possibilities. Why don't you go shower, and I'll make sure the house is secure once Dean returns." Nicole wasn't used to Lia seeming concerned, either. She was typically such a spunky person.

Feeling overwhelmed and a bit short of breath,

Nicole uttered, "Okay," and then added, "Thanks for staying over tonight."

"You know you didn't have much choice in the matter!" Lia grabbed her friend and gave her a quick hug and said, "Goodnight."

When Nicole got into the shower and felt the hot water stream through her hair, she started to cry. For the first time in a long time, she felt afraid for her life.

CHAPTER SIX

"Don't blow this, Dwight. I'm giving you a second chance," said the police chief, Commissioner Melvin Van Stone, before he took a sip out of his coffee mug.

Dwight gritted his teeth, still looking down at his desk at the Rosewood Police Station. Just as he raised his head to meet the commissioner's gaze, however, he forced a Mona Lisa smile. "No, chief. I got this. I think it's the reporter, Danielle Pruitt, and I'm working out the details now."

"What do you mean you think it's the reporter, Danielle Pruitt?" asked the chief with a raised eyebrow.

"Well, she certainly had motive. I heard she hated Stuart since he always got the good articles. And, she certainly doesn't like that owner of the Cannoli Cafe,

Nicole. She has a love interest in Nicole's man, Dean Coogan," Dwight said, triumphantly.

"You listen here, Detective Dawkins. If anything involves Dean, you let me know. And it's not in your job description to make assumptions based on how it would be in a soap opera. You are supposed to be doing a proper investigation, unlike the last time. You hadn't even investigated the library after Frank Tanner was murdered, and look how that turned out! That other library worker almost got killed!"

Detective Dwight Dawkins turned red and stood up to face the chief. "Well, I'm investigating the newspaper and that's how I came up with Danielle as a prime suspect!" answered Dwight with a stern voice.

"Okay, let's talk in the interrogation room. We need to review your next steps." Dwight shook his head as he followed his police chief into the room. The chief motioned for Dwight to sit down. The chief closed the door and sat down across from him. "Tell me your plan." The chief gulped the rest of his coffee and set his mug down hard.

Dwight attempted to compose himself. Swallowing first, he said, "I'm investigating all personnel at the Rosewood Gazette at the moment. I need to meet with June Trainor, Stuart's editor, soon, and I have to meet with Danielle Pruitt as well.

"Wait, what happened to the cafe? Where does that stand in your investigation?"

"Nothing yet. I have toxicology working on it. Also I was thinking of adding Nicole to the suspect list."

"No, there's no reason to add her to the list if we don't find any traces of poison in her cafe."

"Well, that's why I want to get a warrant to search her house. We already have her computer," said Dwight confidently.

"I thought you were just verifying her records in the computer as well as the video surveillance? This is such a mess. I want a thorough, detailed plan of how you're approaching the investigation by this afternoon. You need to sit down and think about this instead of chasing down leads on a whim." The chief was shaking his head. "You have eleven hours. I hope I didn't make a mistake giving you a second chance."

"Why do you care about the cafe so much, chief?" asked Dwight. "To me, Nicole is another prime suspect. After all, she can probably steal a chemical from a lab at the university and slip it into one of her cannolis."

"It's not as easy to steal chemicals as you think. There is a lot of traceability and inventory checks. She doesn't have access to labs, anyway. She teaches thermodynamics, it's a lecture course. That's what I understand from Dean." The commissioner paused. "Dwight, I don't care about the cafe, and I certainly don't like implicating the cafe if there is nothing there. I want you to eliminate suspects and leads if they don't appear credible so we can focus on finding the murderer. Don't waste time. Remember, there is still a killer on the loose. He or she could skip town or slip out from under our noses if we're busy accusing people like Nicole!"

"Well, I think she deserves a little heat. She didn't give me enough time to solve the last case."

The chief jumped out of his chair. "Dawkins, you stop right now. I'm telling you, you're walking a fine line. Get this zipped up and give me a plan by noon. I want that cafe back open by tomorrow so that the community can stop buzzing and hopefully the murderer will come into focus!" The chief grabbed his mug and swung the door so hard it hit the wall.

Dwight sat in his chair another minute, red-faced with his fists clenched.

"Well, Professor, you're not going to get in my way this time. Wait till you see what I have in store for you."

CHAPTER SEVEN

The faint glow of the streetlamp peeked through the slivers of Nicole's window blinds. She groaned as she turned her back to the window once again, frustrated that she woke up for what felt like the millionth time that night. Suddenly, she heard a light tap on her door.

"It's just me," said Lia, walking in with two mugs of chamomile tea on a breakfast tray. Nicole sat up in bed once she saw her friend, propping the pillow behind her back. "Mind if I join you for a few minutes? It's 2 a.m. and I know you're not sleeping well." Lia set the tray down in front of her friend and proceeded to sit in the armchair next to Nicole's bed.

Nicole gave her dear friend a small smile. "Thanks. How did you know?"

"I heard you talking in your sleep. Tell me what's

bothering you the most." Just then Nicole heard a car drive by. Before Nicole could speak, Lia read her mind and said, "Dean already brought your car back and returned your key, so don't worry about that."

"Oh, that's great. Thank goodness for good friends. You and Dean—" Nicole's voice trailed off, a tear going down her face. Lia took her hand and nodded to her. Encouraged to voice her concerns, Nicole answered, "I'm just worried. What if I missed something? What if I took my eye off the ball and somehow someone did slip something into the kitchen? Maybe I got too comfortable here. Maybe I was enjoying my life too much, too fast here in Rosewood. Back in industry... if I took my eye off someone for a second they would sense it and sneak in the attack."

"Nicole, this isn't industry. And you have the surveillance cameras. The police will be able to confirm all that once they are through with your computer." Lia took her hand back so she could cradle her mug of tea with both hands and sip it. Nicole mirrored her friend and took a sip from hers as well, not realizing she was being led unconsciously. She was in such a worried state she couldn't get beyond the concerns in her mind.

They sat in silence for a moment, both continuing to drink in the warmth. Nicole set her tea down as her eyes fluttered. "This tea helped, thank you. I'm feeling a bit sleepy now. I think my body is about to give out."

"Here, let me take that before you get another second wind. Put your head down." Nicole let go of worrying for the moment, perhaps due to the comfort of her friend's presence, and drifted off to sleep. She had a big day ahead in terms of sleuthing.

At 8 a.m. Nicole's alarm rang. *I don't remember setting that*, she thought. When she went to turn it off, she saw a note taped to it: *Glad you were able to rest. Good luck today at the library.*

Nicole smiled at her friend's note and stretched as she stood up. She pulled on her pink robe and considered how it really was deja vu after all. She first felt that familiar tingle the previous night at the cafe, and again she found herself waking up in her house, thinking about a murder, while Lia was staying with her and leaving her notes. The only difference was that her cafe was being implicated this time. She shuddered at the thought and put her slippers on, heading to the kitchen to get coffee.

While she enjoyed using her French Press many mornings, she knew her stomach wouldn't be able to handle it that particular morning. She had noticed that the retention of the coffee oils through the use of the French Press upset her stomach at times, and with her stomach already being in knots, she figured it wouldn't be a good idea to press her luck. She had recently acquired a single-cup machine and decided to try that instead. She selected an organic coffee pod and retrieved her motivational mug from the cabinet. "I need all the help I can get today," she said to herself. The mug read: *Believe*.

Once her coffee was brewed, she added creamer and continued to talk to herself. "This is an instant type of morning." She bent down and found some instant oatmeal in her pantry. She was waiting for the microwave to cook the oats with water when she suddenly heard a noise in the living room.

"Ringo! I'm so sorry, I'm out of sorts this morning." Ringo didn't seem to mind Nicole's distracted state. She saw his water bowl looked full as well as the one for his food. "Lia, thank goodness," she said to herself. "Ringo, I bet Aunt Lia took you out earlier but you probably want to run around some more." She opened the door that led to her beautifully land-scaped fenced yard and admired the black lab. He looked so free as he started to run through the grass.

She pulled her patio blinds open so she could watch Ringo more easily while eating her breakfast.

She figured she had a little time to compose herself before going to the library, especially since it would not be opening until 10 a.m. It was going to be a big research day since she was going to check all the past articles of Stuart Helm's from the last year, searching for clues as to who might have been interested in murdering him. Just then her phone rang.

"Hi Susie, how are you...yes, I believe we have to remain closed...I'll call you once I get the green light that we can re-open...I am hanging in there, don't worry about me...Thanks for calling...Bye now." She hung up and finished her remaining coffee and oatmeal. Then she stood up and peered out the front window, observing that Dean had indeed returned her car as Lia said.

Feeling grateful and cared for, she decided to send Dean a text message: *Good morning. Thanks for returning my car last night. Appreciate any insight about when I can re-open...I'm a wreck about this.*

She felt a little awkward about the last sentence, but she was trying to be open in her relationship with Dean. It was a challenge for her to be vulnerable, but she knew she didn't have a chance with him if she kept her feelings hidden.

When she didn't get an immediate response, she decided to let Ringo back in so she could take a shower and get ready for the library. She was hoping to receive some good news, that she could return to her cafe right after the library if luck were on her side. "Let's hope," she said to herself as she laid out her clothes on the bed.

Nicole peered through the glass door to the main foyer of the library. Taking a deep breath, she mentally psyched herself up for the task ahead and pulled the right handle toward her. As she crossed the threshold, she again experienced that feeling of deja vu, recalling that the previous library director, Frank Tanner, was murdered; her last visit to the library, in an effort to help solve that murder, was not exactly pleasant. "Here we go again," Nicole muttered under her breath. Upon entering the sunny vestibule, Christina Morano, the new library director, walked up to Nicole and gave her a warm embrace.

"Hi Nicole. How *are* you? Are you okay?" Christina asked.

"Christina," was all Nicole could muster for a reply at first. Christina's hug seemed to unlock Nicole's emotions a bit. She felt as if her overwhelm was about to escape, that she couldn't control it. She tried to swallow back that feeling in the throat when one needs to cry.

Christina rubbed Nicole's arm as she gently pulled back. "I heard all about what happened. Dan and I are very worried about you. We want to help as much as we can. I suspect you're here to do some research, that you're 'on the case again' as they say! Let me guess, you want to look through Stuart Helm's articles for clues?"

Nicole nodded, feeling grateful for the gesture of support. "Yes, that's exactly why I'm here." She thought about how Christina might be able to help her here in the library while her husband Dan, interestingly enough, was helping her indirectly by managing her aunt's restaurant, and doing a great job of it from what she could tell.

"Let's go to the back room. I got in early and was able to isolate a lot of his writing from the past year, particularly the pieces that were more major. I also noted articles that implicated other individuals in them. You know, where someone may have been offended by his writing!"

As the two women walked through the back hallway, Nicole breathed a sigh of relief. She smiled warmly at Christina and said, "Great minds think alike. I really appreciate your help. I didn't expect to make sleuthing a habit and this time I'm truly caught off-guard with my own cafe being wrapped up in the whole thing, especially with that Detective Dawkins seeming so fixated on it."

Christina and Nicole arrived at the back room. Newspapers covered the main table, with more newspapers stacked and resting on one of the chairs. "Is he? Interesting you mention him. I have the articles related to Frank Tanner's murder right here, and they do seem to imply that he didn't do his job properly. I bet he's trying to fix his image in this case and make up for his errors!" said Christina.

"Yes, I suppose that's a natural reaction. And Stuart *was* holding a cannoli when he was found. I guess the detective needs to do his due diligence this time since he didn't even bother to investigate properly the last time. He wasn't even the detective who apprehended the last murderer!" Nicole noticed that Christina shook her head a bit at her last remark but didn't comment further, seeming distracted as she paged through the papers on the table. "What about articles that were completely unrelated to Frank Tanner's murder?" Nicole asked, rubbing her chin in thought.

Christina gulped. "I hope the mob doesn't have ears everywhere, but you know Stuart did write an article about how the Rosewood Coffee Shoppe was going downhill since you took over the Cannoli Cafe."

"I'm sorry, what does that have to do with the mob?" asked Nicole.

"Well, the owner of Rosewood Coffee Shoppe is Bert Davison, close friend of alleged mob associate Vincent Mongelli!" Christina explained, seeming very excited. "In fact, rumor has it that the coffee shop may be a front for the mob, that they often use his private room downstairs. Word on the street is that the location is at the center for a lot of 'deals' so-to-speak."

"Oh, dear!" Nicole felt her pulse quicken. She vaguely remembered Lia mentioning that article to her, but she didn't think much of it. She hadn't under-stood the subtlety of what that meant. The last thing she wanted was to be a mob target. "I wonder if they wanted to kill two birds with one stone. Improve business for Bert and get rid of the guy who wrote that his cafe was on the decline."

Christina's eyes widened. "Honestly, Dan and I were up half the night talking about that possibility. Dan knows how they work. He's got cousins involved in that world, if you know what I mean. He never wanted any part of it so he's led an honest life, working for your aunt, you know. But if there's one thing he does know; he knows you *don't* want to get on their radar."

Nicole stopped leaning over the table with

Christina and pulled up an empty chair, feeling a little woozy. She put her head in her hands and said, "I suppose I'm lucky to be alive then! What a mess! My cafe is closed, and its reputation—not to mention mine—is probably ruined. And there is a murderer on the loose!" She closed her eyes and remained still.

Alarmed, Christina said, "Nicole, I've never quite seen you like this before. It's going to be okay. If anyone can figure this out, it's you. And maybe the murderer isn't in the mob. Maybe if you figure out who it is soon, this will all come to an end."

"I certainly hope so. If it's the mob, I'm doomed, because then it means I'm on their radar. On second thought, if the Cannoli Cafe goes downhill as a result of all this, then I probably won't be a target anymore. But all my plans will be ruined." Sighing, Nicole shuffled through some of the other articles on the table and said, "Christina, did anything else stick out? Any other possibilities?"

Just then there was a knock on the door. A fresh, young face poked through the doorway. "May I come in? Hi, Professor. Hello, Mrs. Morano," greeted Sarah, an assistant in the library. Sarah played a key role in the last murder in town. She was also a student of Nicole's at the University of New Jersey.

Christina Morano looked at Nicole to ensure there was no objection and motioned for Sarah to come in. "Nicole, I hope you don't mind, but Sarah was in early helping me with the article curation. She actually pulled the articles from the archives so that you wouldn't have to search on microfiche. They were all from the past few months, anyway."

"That's wonderful, I really do appreciate the support from you both."

"It was no trouble, Professor. I actually wanted to talk with you about an issue that came up at school recently. I think it might be connected to the murder." Christina and Nicole looked at each other with wide eyes.

"Please, do go ahead," said Nicole, eager to identify another suspect, perhaps one without "associates."

"Mrs. Morano, we didn't initially set aside this article because it involved a high school student, but I think the professor should know about it. Gregory Gornick is a student I tutor occasionally. His father, the business administrator, is very high-powered in town. He prides himself on being an Ivy League graduate and wanted his son to do the same. But Stuart Helm wrote an article about how Gregory cheated on an exam, so Gregory's acceptance was revoked at the colleges he applied to, which were all Ivy League actually."

"Are you saying you think Tom Gornick could be a suspect?" asked Nicole.

"Yes, but please don't tell anyone I'm saying this, since he sometimes employs me to help Gregory. But I have a bad feeling about it. Gregory told me his father is furious about the article and that he was going to find a way to get back at him, especially since they've had issues in the past."

"What issues?" asked Christina.

"I don't know, honestly. Gregory said he couldn't say more on that. All he could tell me was that they had some sort of bad history."

"Thanks so much, Sarah. I think I will pay a visit to Mr. Gornick. After all, I still work at the university. Maybe I can offer some help in terms of his college options and see what I can find out in the process."

Nicole quickly looked at her phone since she thought she heard it beep while Sarah was talking. She saw the message was from Dean and was eager to find out if she could re-open her cafe. After saying goodbye to Christina and Sarah, she opened her phone to see: *No go. Call me when you can.*

"Oh my, I guess I won't be re-opening quite yet," Nicole said to herself.

CHAPTER EIGHT

One week prior to the murder

"Can't you just take care of the girl?" pleaded Bert Davison, owner of the Rosewood Coffee Shoppe. He was sitting across from his best friend, Vincent Mongelli, an alleged associate of the Donati "family."

"I'm not going to do it, Bert. First of all, the boss doesn't want to get into that anymore. It was different in the '30s and '40s. But now it's easier to get caught, and you get too much time if they nail you. It's messy. We're focusing on jobs and services only, and we have other ways to get what we want," answered Vincent in a thick New Jersey-New York metropolitan accent.

Vincent took a big gulp of his coffee, draining his

mug. The Rosewood Coffee Shoppe had a front counter setup, similar to a New Jersey diner, where patrons could order food or coffee. Vincent was sitting on a stool at the counter in a completely empty establishment.

"Jobs and services? What ways? What the heck are you talking about?" asked Bert.

"You know, construction, garbage, etc. Stuff people need and can't do without. We want to control as much of it as we can. Besides, I don't want Lucia's niece to get hurt."

Bert sighed, his eyes gazing over the empty tables and chairs.

Vince shook his head and then handed him his coffee mug. Bert grabbed the coffee pot from behind the counter and gave him a refill before returning the mug. "Something tells me you're not telling me everything. What's this about Lucia? I thought the Capulas were clean. She's not linked to you guys at all," Bert said.

"Lucia *is* clean. All of the Capulas are. Look, she's a nice lady who has a great restaurant and good food."

"Sounds like you're interested—"

"Cut it out, Bert. What do you want me to do? You can't blame people for wanting to go to Nicole's cafe. She's got a pretty face and a nice personality, which is more than I can say for you. And the cannolis are to die for!" said Vincent in a raised voice.

"To die for...yeah," mumbled Bert.

"Bert, I was in there the other day. She's got the old men there for the chess club one night. Then she's got the old women there many mornings doing their knitting, sipping on tea and coffee, and eating pastries. They sit there for hours and just keep eating. She's even got the young crowd coming in sometimes. It's the place to be."

Bert banged his fist against the counter. "Darn it, I need to do something fast, Vincent. Ever since that Stuart Helm wrote his article about that place we've tanked. I don't get it. He's not even a food critic but he went and wrote that piece about how interesting it was that a Ph.D. chemical engineer turned into a cafe owner and then business started drying up! And once she solved that murder, forget it! Everyone stopped coming here," Bert said, gritting his teeth, his fists still clenched from when he hit the counter.

"Ah, when you put it that way she does sound a lot more interesting than you! So I don't see what you need me for then." Vincent stood up and buttoned his black suit jacket.

Bert was silent for a moment as he looked down at the floor, scratching his heavily receded hairline. "Her cannolis are really to die for, Vince?"

"Without a doubt, why?"

"Good. I have an idea."

"I don't want to hurt Nicole, Bert—" warned Vincent.

"No no, she may get a little scratch in the pocket-book, that's all. I promise," said Bert.

Vincent gave Bert a quizzical look. "Explain it to me."

"We're going to throw that Stuart Helm off. In fact, we're going to give him a gift he can't forget. This will *guarantee* more business for the Rosewood Coffee Shoppe." In a hoarse whisper, despite the empty shoppe, Bert said, "Here's what we're gonna do. I need you to deliver something for me next week to Stuart. As the saying goes, sometimes it's best to 'kill 'em with kindness!'" said Bert with a half-smile.

CHAPTER NINE

Nicole sighed as her body surrendered to the car seat cushions. Leaning back, she closed her eyes and pushed her head back gently into the headrest. "I can't believe this," she said to herself.

A sharp *knock, knock, knock* startled her to full attention. "Wake up, Dr. Capula!" yelled a familiar voice.

"Lia!" Nicole saw her friend banging on the passenger window. She promptly exited her vehicle and went up to her friend.

"What are you doing here outside my practice?"

Nicole thought about how she had spoken with Dean on the phone while she was still in the library parking lot. He explained that the police did not find any cause for concern in their preliminary investigation. The labs would be back by the end of the day, and if nothing was found, she could reopen her cafe the next day. That was the good news.

The bad news was that the business administrator and head of the Downtown Management Team, Thomas Gornick, had objections to her reopening so soon. Feeling so drained and even a bit dizzy, she didn't even have the energy to articulate all that to her friend, yet she had driven directly to Lia's practice to seek her advice. "I need your help," Nicole answered.

Lia took Nicole by the arm and led her inside to her office. "Dean called me after speaking with you. He was worried about how strained you sounded on the phone. Here, sit down."

"He did?" Nicole accepted a cup of water that Lia handed her.

"Yes. To be honest, I'm a little concerned, too. I've never seen you like this."

"My chest is hurting a little. I think it's anxiety." Nicole sipped at the water, her hand rubbing the top of her chest, just under her neck."

"When was the last time you had a checkup?" asked Lia.

"Not in a while. But I have noticed occasional bouts of dizziness and chest pain. They were sporadic before, but I've been feeling a lot worse today. I feel so embarrassed."

"Embarrassed? What if you have a real medical problem? I'm taking you to Dr. Covington right now. I'll call Dan and cancel the pizza." Lia picked up the phone receiver from her desk and started dialing. Nicole stood up and promptly took the receiver from Lia and returned it to its base.

"I promise I'll get checked in the next few days. I sometimes get this when I need to eat. What did you say about pizza?"

Lia, with furrowed brows, answered, "I'm glad you finally told me what's been on your mind. Remember the other night in the cafe? I knew something was up with you."

"Well, actually it's almost like I had a premonition that night, sort of a gut instinct, that something bad was about to happen. Kind of strange." Nicole shook her head before continuing. "But yes, this issue was in the back of my mind as well. Now, about the pizza?"

Lia laughed, "I suppose you really are hungry! I called Dan at your aunt's restaurant and asked if someone could bring a margarita pizza over. I noticed you sitting in your car without moving for a few minutes and figured you needed fortification! I also ordered a side of meatballs. You know, to keep up your strength!"

"Thanks, you're a good friend." The two women

smiled at each other. "Lia—" started Nicole, before a tapping noise at the front door interrupted her.

"That must be the pizza," said Lia.

"Hello, ladies!" Dan Morano walked into Lia's practice, bearing a steamy box of pizza along with an insulated bag with the words "Lucia's Trattoria" imprinted on it, presumably with the meatballs inside.

"Smells delicious! Hi Dan!" said Nicole. Lia accepted the pizza and meatballs and started to set up paper plates at her desk.

"Nicole, how are you doing? Is there anything I can do for you? I heard about what happened," said Dan in a concerned tone.

"Thanks, Dan. Actually your wife was very helpful at the library. I was doing some research just before —" Nicole's voice trailed off while she thought about how Sarah, an assistant at the library, had walked in at the end and talked about her concerns with regard to Thomas Gornick. And now Thomas Gornick was the one stopping her from reopening the Cannoli Cafe.

"I have a confession to make, ladies. I am delivering this personally because I overheard Thomas Gornick talking with other members of the Downtown Management Team over lunch at the restaurant. He wants to keep you closed until the investigation is over. Oh, please go ahead and start," said Dan as he gestured toward the pizza.

"I know, that's why I'm so upset right now. Some murder investigations take months!" Nicole took a bite from her slice.

"Listen, Nicole, this guy Gornick is all bite. He puts on an act but is quick to cower when he's confronted. There was a time he tried to shut Lucia down and she wasn't having it! He tried to say that she was running a mob establishment simply because Vincent Mongelli ate there sometimes! Gornick never bothered her again after she was done arguing with him!"

Nicole glanced at Lia, curious if she picked up on the remark about Vincent Mongelli. She hadn't yet explained to her some of the insight she gained at the library, that perhaps the murder and cafe framing was driven by Vincent or his friend Bert from the Rosewood Coffee Shoppe. Lia's eyebrows gave the slightest twitch when their eyes briefly met.

Nicole's eyes widened. "Dan, did you say anything to my aunt about what happened? Has she called?"

Dan offered a warm smile. "No, don't worry. She did call, but we all know how much she needs to rest. I figured you'd want to tell her yourself when the time is right. But I do think you should take a page out of your aunt's book, that's my two-cents. She may be getting up in years, as we've seen recently with her heart and all, but she's still got it, you know? She doesn't let anyone get away with *anything*!"

Nicole smiled at Dan's words. He was right. Though her aunt was starting to show some signs of physical weakness, she possessed a certain strength on the inside. "Lia, Dan's right. Maybe I should pay a visit to this Thomas Gornick after lunch."

"And I'll join you. They were talking about how they wanted to diversify and add members to that Downtown Management Team and had approached me about joining."

"Good idea, Lia. I'm glad you will be joining me." Nicole took another bite of her pizza, feeling relieved that she at least had a plan.

Lia winked. "No problem. Might be a great opportunity to 'kill two birds with one stone.'"

Nicole shook her head before saying to Dan, "She loves that phrase."

After Lia and Nicole saved the leftover pizza and meatballs in Lia's office refrigerator, they proceeded to walk out of her practice and in the direction of the town hall. Rosewood was quite pretty this time of year, with the end of spring and warmer months of summer beginning. Nicole took a deep breath of the fresh air, noting the fullness of the trees dotting the sidewalk.

"Nervous?" asked Lia, glancing at her friend.

"A little. I remember he was a bit difficult to deal with when I first took over the cafe. Lots of questions and not very friendly. I got the impression he thinks he's better than all of us, or at least me." Nicole clenched her fists in anticipation of the difficult conversation. After all, how was she going to approach it? If she appeared too friendly, he would walk all over her and not take her seriously. If she seemed too serious and direct, he could match her attitude. It seemed to be a "no-win" situation in her view.

Lia put a hand on Nicole's shoulder before saying, "Well, here goes." She held the door for her friend and ushered her in first. They walked down the main corridor of the town hall. Nicole remembered that Thomas Gornick's office was to the right, around the corner. Nicole motioned her head to the right and Lia nodded. As they rounded the corner, Nicole walked straight into Thomas.

"I'm so sorry, Mr. Gornick. I didn't realize you were right there."

"You should watch where you're going!" he

answered. "What are you doing here anyway? I hope you didn't come here to see me."

"As a matter of fact, we *are* here to see you," piped up Lia. Thomas Gornick hadn't even seemed to notice Lia until she spoke up. "Remember Diane Eckel had approached me about joining the Downtown Management Team? Well, I didn't receive more information, and yet I heard there was a lunch meeting today. I came to provide my input on the situation and make sure you know to include me next time."

Gornick's face turned into what appeared to be a square jaw. "What situation? If you're talking about your friend's cafe, well you are a bit biased now, aren't you?"

"Aren't you speaking about yourself, sir?" said Nicole. "What do you have against my cafe anyway?"

"I am the business administrator, and I have the final word on this. Your cafe should not reopen until the investigation is complete!" yelled Gornick.

"The investigation will be complete on my cafe within a few hours. If all the labs show my establishment is clean, that there are no traces of poison, then I don't understand your justification!"

"You think you're so smart with your goody-two-shoes personality and on top of that your ridiculous Ph.D. That degree means nothing, not when it's from the University of New Jersey! People like you, the ones who claim all you need to do is 'work hard with what you've got' are ruining the historical systems we private school alumni have put in place! We have established networks for a reason! You're just 'Nicole Nobody!' Nobody important, for sure!"

"That's Dr. Capula to *you*, sir. And how did this become personal? I run a business. I don't see what my background or life has to do with anything!" Nicole was fuming at this point, and Lia was watching with her jaw wide-open.

"That's enough!" Mayor Diane Eckel emerged from her office, which was a few feet away from where they were arguing in the hallway. "Tom, this is ridiculous. First of all, I think you're too emotional from the situation with your son still. Take the rest of the week off, and that's an order. And since I have the ultimate authority, especially while you're gone, Dr. Capula's cafe will reopen as soon as the police clear it. There is no substantial reason otherwise!"

Thomas Gornick huffed and straightened his suit jacket before turning around and entering his office.

The mayor put a hand on Nicole's arm and whispered, "I'm not sure what's come over him. Ever since that article about his son was published, he's been very edgy, and more focused on private versus public universities to boot. I don't understand it. I had suggested that he speak with you about his son's situation and he got very upset with me!"

"That's odd. Yes, I might have been able to help there." Nicole was shaking just a touch, feeling rattled from the argument she had with the business administrator. "Well, I'm so glad you were here to help, Mayor Eckel."

"It's no problem, Nicole. You know, I never got to apologize for running away from you and Dean during the last murder case. I was very upset. By now I'm sure you've heard the history. But things are going well for my son, and he's actually been included in some of the family events now that everyone understands who is father really was. Things are so much easier now that everything is out in the open."

"That's wonderful," said Lia. "I didn't realize that it was all out in the open."

"Yes, a story for another time. Maybe I can share it with you both over cappuccinos, when the Cannoli Cafe is reopened. After all, I'd like to get to know you two better. You are the youngest downtown business owners in Rosewood, and I want to get you both more integrated into our community. We have to keep our small-town economy flourishing, and I believe you both play important parts in that."

"Speaking of which, I'm actually expecting a client shortly and need to get back," said Lia.

Nicole nodded. "And I want to get in touch with Susie so that we can be on track to reopen as soon as possible. Thank you so much, Mayor Eckel, for your help."

"Please, you can both call me Diane. Take care now. Oh, and Nicole? My office will be in touch. We'll be providing dessert and coffee at a few future events, and I wouldn't mind featuring your cannolis and pastries going forward!" said the Mayor with a broad smile.

CHAPTER TEN

"He'd better be bringing wine!" said Lia.

"He probably will, don't worry! Here, can you set the table for me?" Nicole handed Lia three dishes.

"Forks and knives?" asked Lia. "And why *don't* you have any wine?"

"I'm sorry, I'm still thinking about the odd exchange we had with Thomas Gornick earlier." Nicole opened the kitchen drawer and removed six utensils in total. She handed them to Lia.

"Ah, I figured the wheels might be turning in your head, unlike Ringo at the moment. Look at him enjoying his bed near the fireplace. He's at peace and doesn't have to worry about such matters!" said Lia as she walked through the pocket-door opening to the dining room.

Nicole liked that her ranch had the convenience

of one-floor living yet it also had a traditional feel. She found the dining room to be quite charming since it had a rounded archway leading to the living room, allowing her to extend the table several times over when needed (a must for her Italian-American extended family on holidays!). Not to mention that she adored her fireplace in the living room.

Nicole took a deep breath, an attempt to calm her nerves after the trying day, and heard the sound of utensils clanking against the table. When Lia returned to the kitchen, Nicole said, "To answer your question, I got out of the habit of buying wine, since Dean typically brings it himself. Besides, I mostly drink it when I have company."

"Aha, the truth comes out. You're becoming dependent on him!" Lia smiled broadly as she waved her finger in the air.

"Please stop, you silly accountant!" Nicole jested.

Lia shook her head. "I'm asking because I've been looking into that Mediterranean diet. Maybe we should try that, a glass of red wine each night. Like true Italians! You know, if I move in here I would establish that rule."

Nicole gave her friend a quizzical look. "What makes you think you're moving in?"

"Maybe we should think about it. This is the

second murder you're involved in this year and you need my support!"

Nicole chuckled at her friend. "You're right, I do need your support. But your house is just around the corner! Besides, I think the coincidence of my return in the last year along with the rise in Rosewood murders is a fluke. I bet this will be the last one I'll be involved in."

Lia lifted one eyebrow in the direction of her friend. "Maybe. Well, I like having my house as a write-off anyway, though I could always rent it!" Lia glanced at the oven. "How much longer? Smells delicious!"

"Glad that's settled, for now." Nicole placed three wine glasses on her kitchen counter. She was also hoping that Dean would be supplying wine for their dinner, just to help her relax a little. She liked keeping her wits about her, but she was feeling frustrated that her cafe was still closed and caught up in the case. She hoped if she were a touch more relaxed she might have a revelation or new perspective. "We should focus on dinner and making progress on our suspect list. I'm making the Italian Baked Macaroni dish I had served the other night at the cafe. You know, that night the police came in! I never got a chance to sample it myself with everything going on!

It's ready, but I'll keep it on the 'keep warm' setting until Dean arrives."

Suddenly, Ringo seemingly jumped out of his slumber and started barking. The doorbell rang, and Nicole looked over at Lia.

"Must be your boyfriend. I'll get it!" said Lia as she walked through the other pocket door that led directly to the living room, parallel to the dining room archway.

"I've been thinking about that, too, and I prefer the term 'beau,'" shouted Nicole. Just then, Dean walked into her house with a wine bottle and flowers in hand.

"For me? Oh, thank you, Dean," said Lia. Ringo jumped between Lia and Dean, eager to see Nicole's "beau," and ready for some attention.

"Not exactly, Lia," chuckled Dean. His glasses slid down his nose a bit as he patted Ringo. "Hi, boy, are you keeping Nicole safe?"

Nicole walked over to receive her wine and flowers. She kissed him on the cheek. "Thank you for the wine and this stunning bouquet. How beautiful!" She took his arm and led him to the dining area. She went over to the china closet, removed a vase and then headed to the kitchen sink to fill it with water. She then carefully unwrapped the gorgeous mix of white lilies and red roses and placed them inside the crystal vase.

"Beautiful!" whispered Lia to herself, almost wistfully. She grabbed the bottle of wine from the dining room. "Ah, I'll take care of the wine," said Lia with a wink. She brought it to the kitchen. "Oh a screw top! And a Chianti! This should be good!" She proceeded to pour the luscious red liquid into the three waiting glasses.

After placing the vase on the buffet table, Nicole turned around and hugged Dean. "Thank you again."

"Ahem," said Lia, clearing her throat. Nicole and Dean stepped away from one another, each accepting their wine glasses. They clinked while Lia proposed, "To solving the case!" They each took a sip and nodded to one another.

"Why don't you both sit down. I'll get the macaroni from the oven!" said Nicole. She used her oven mitts to carefully remove a 9x13 glass dish. The cheese was still bubbling a bit as she placed the heavy dish full of homemade tomato gravy, ground beef, macaroni, mozzarella and parmesan on a trivet in the dining room. She proceeded to serve Lia and Dean first before putting some on her plate also.

"There's Italian bread in the basket. Also, I placed the salad on the table, but I usually eat it after the main dish."

"I've been wondering about that, actually. Is that an Italian thing?" asked Dean. Nicole's eye caught his hand rubbing his forehead, a nervous habit he exhibited when he was worried or stressed.

"The salad after the meal? I never really thought about it. My family always did it. And I've eaten with Nicole's and I know it's a tradition for them, too." Lia, whose name is the Italian version of *Leah* from the Bible, grew up in the same culture as Nicole—one of the reasons they could relate to each other quite well growing up in Rosewood.

"Yes, my parents and grandparents always said it was supposed to help with digestion. But why are we talking about salad, Dean?" Nicole swallowed a forkful of her macaroni.

"I guess I can't hide much from you, Nicole. I know we're really here tonight to discuss the murder of Stuart Helm. But I can't stop thinking about how you could have been killed in the last murder investigation." Dean paused. "I don't want to lose you. I think we should let the police handle this one."

Nicole took a sip of her wine. "I don't know, Dean. I'm worried that Detective Dawkins will botch this investigation, just like he did the last time. I think we should continue finding out what we can."

"But what if something happens to you? Promise me you won't approach any suspects by yourself, please? Once you find something, contact the police," pleaded Dean.

Before Nicole could answer, Lia piped up, "Dean, I feel awkward asking this, but what do you do as a private investigator? Why is Nicole the one looking into things?"

"I know why you're asking. I'm not officially on this case. I have to be careful not to overstep the Rosewood Police Department since they hire me for various jobs. Other local police departments hire me as well. I'm sort of like a law enforcement consultant."

"Can you give me an example?" asked Lia.

"I can't say too much. Confidentiality and all. But I can help with things ranging from tracking down debtors to setting up surveillance on someone. Depends on the client's needs. That's in the private sector. But police departments sometimes need help managing cases. Sometimes they will have an over-flow of burglaries and then they will ask me to inves-tigate a few of them."

"Interesting. So did you talk to anyone in the Rosewood Police today?" asked Lia.

"Yes, as a matter of fact, Commissioner Van Stone did share some information even though I'm not officially involved." He looked cautiously over to Nicole. She suspected he really did not want to share the information, since it would spur her to take the next logical steps in investigating whatever he was about to share. She nodded and smiled in encouragement. "He mentioned Danielle Pruitt had purchased cannolis the day prior to the murder based on the video surveillance recorded in the program on Nicole's computer. He said Detective Dawkins seemed *very* focused on her, but they also noticed Vincent Mongelli had purchased cannolis as well."

"Oh no!" said Nicole in a noticeably heavy tone.

"What is it?" asked Dean.

"I understand he is a friend of Bert Davison's. Stuart had written an article basically trashing his coffee shoppe and praising my cafe. After finding that out at the library today, I've been worrying that I could be a mob target."

Dean took in Nicole's words while rubbing his forehead again.

"What about Thomas Gornick, Dean? Wait until you hear about the crazy conversation we had with *him* this afternoon!" said Lia. She promptly took another large forkful of her macaroni.

"Funny, he mentioned Gornick as a perfect example of someone who wouldn't be a suspect! That was part of the problem with the surveillance, he explained, that so many people bought cannolis in the twenty-four hours prior to the murder—they'd have a suspect list of at least fifty people!"

"Well he's a suspect in my book, but what do I know!" said Lia.

Nicole was still thinking about Dean's comment on the surveillance. "Interesting about Danielle Pruitt on the video. That's on top of the fact that she found Stuart—dead. She could have been jealous of his success and wanted him out of the way at the paper. She's definitely a suspect. Second is Vincent Mongelli, possibly acting on behalf of Bert Davison. And after seeing Thomas Gornick's anger towards me, I would say he should be added to the list as well. I agree with you, Lia." Nicole's eyes glistened over.

Dean took her hand from across the table. "What did he say to you?"

"He seems to have a personal vendetta against me, but I can't figure out why. He tried to discredit my Ph.D. from the University of New Jersey, and he called me 'Nicole Nobody.'" A tear ran down Nicole's face.

Dean promptly stood up, "Why that—" Lia and Nicole looked at one another with their jaws slightly open. It wasn't like Dean to exhibit so much anger. He couldn't even get any words out. Dean shook his head and sat back down. "Yes, add him to the list.

And please don't go near him again! Why did you see him anyway?"

"It was two-fold. One was that he didn't want my cafe to reopen until the investigation was completely over, which could be months! The other was that Stuart Helm had apparently written a shaming article about his son, Gregory, who cheated on an exam at the high school. As a result, colleges may rescind Gregory's acceptance, especially at some of those elite schools. You know Thomas Gornick won't want him to attend a state school, given his attitude. Especially after what I witnessed today."

"Interesting. We should hear something before the morning about whether you can reopen. They were waiting on the last lab analysis."

Nicole nodded. "Dean, about the investigation— did the chief mention anything about what Stuart had been working on before he died? I'm starting to wonder if we are looking in the wrong place. Maybe we should be focusing on what he was about to write? Maybe there was something he was about to publish that the murderer wanted to remain hidden?"

"You do have a good mind for crime, Nicole, I have to say. Unfortunately, the murderer destroyed his computer and the tech guys say it's unrecoverable," said Dean.

"Oh no! That's terrible. What about my computer? Any news on when I can get that back?"

"I heard that Dawkins wants to hang on to it for a few days, even though the cafe is reopening. He wants to make sure they didn't miss anything with the video footage."

"That gives me an idea. Maybe I'll stop by the university tomorrow. I'm not teaching this summer semester, but I do have some work I'll need to prepare for the department, and I need a computer for that. Maybe while I'm there I'll talk with my friend Gabriel, head of Information Technology, and see what he thinks about the recoverability of a computer, just out of curiosity."

"This macaroni is delicious, Nicole. I'm sorry I didn't mention it earlier—I was so caught up with all the murder talk," said Lia. Dean nodded with a full mouth and also had an empty plate.

Nicole quickly rose from the table, grabbed a few salad plates from her counter, and returned to the dining room. "Help yourself to the salad. I'll take the dirty plates." As she cleared part of the table, her gaze fell on Ringo across in the living room, who seemed to be at peace again next to the fire. *I'm glad someone can rest easily in this house*, she thought to herself.

CHAPTER ELEVEN

"Ladies, why in the world are we *here* this morning? I thought we agreed we don't want to share the same fate as Stuart Helm!" said Mary in a very loud whisper.

"Mary!" pleaded Doris, the head of Knitting for Good—an organization that was made up of some of the more senior ladies of the Rosewood community. "Shush! As I said by telephone chain, the police cleared this place. There were no traces of poison whatsoever. Nicole's cannolis must have been tainted after they were purchased here."

"I'm the last person on the chain, and the message I heard was that we we're all gonna die this morning," said Charlotte quite matter-of-factly. A soft-spoken member, she always had a knack for saying the most surprising remarks despite her gentle nature. Nicole, naturally, was cringing as she listened to the entire conversation from the front counter. Susie overheard, too, and put her hand on Nicole's arm.

"Don't worry, sweetie. At least they came this morning!" said Susie in her usual warm voice.

Nicole turned her head and smiled at her baker (and manager in Nicole's absence). "Notice they haven't eaten anything."

Susie shrugged. "It'll pass in time. I did notice a few ladies sipping their tea. Once there is some new gossip, they'll go back to plotting about the next romantic affair in town while knitting baby blankets for charity!"

Nicole let out a hearty laugh at the remark, so loud that the ladies stopped and looked over at her. She thought she heard someone whisper, "How can she be so cheerful?" Nicole made a face at Susie and ducked into the kitchen. All the way in the back corner was her own personal cubicle of sorts. She had a desk where she normally kept her computer, a chair, and a personal refrigerator—she didn't like mixing personal with business (unless her baked goods were about go to stale, then she made an exception). She took a breath while she thought about how challenging the morning was. Everything had gotten stale in their absence so she and Susie were there bright and early baking new batches of cookies and cannolis.

Nicole eyed her empty workstation and thought about how she couldn't program her security cameras without her computer. *I definitely need to see Gabriel at the university; maybe he could suggest a temporary solution,* she thought to herself.

Just as she was about to pack her bag and head to campus, Susie came in. "Danielle Pruitt is here egging on the Knitting for Good ladies. She is scaring them off this minute!"

Alarmed, Nicole immediately left the kitchen and went into the main area of the cafe.

"No, I don't feel safe eating here. I purchased tea to appear supportive since Nicole lets our group sit here and knit for charity several mornings a week typically. But maybe we should switch to the Rosewood Coffee Shoppe, as you're suggesting," said Mary.

"Mary! Shush!" said Doris.

Nicole approached the person instigating the conversation, Danielle Pruitt. She figured she would start with kindness and see where it went. "Excuse me, can I help you?" she asked.

Danielle, a spiky-haired, petite woman, most

likely in her late 20s, said, "Yes, I'm here to do a follow-up story on what happened to my colleague, Stuart Helm. How do you feel about your cafe being so empty this morning?" asked the reporter.

"It's not empty. Knitting for Good is here—" answered Nicole.

"But they're afraid to eat. Or drink."

"I'm sorry, but aren't you a main suspect? Why aren't you at the police station? I thought you found Stuart's dead body," challenged Nicole.

The expression on Danielle's face matched Nicole's tone. "I simply found him. There's no evidence I poisoned him. Besides, someone needs to follow-up on all these stories now." Danielle half-smiled.

Nicole's brows furrowed. She knew about the video camera footage but didn't want to say anything. Maybe the police had not approached her about that yet, after all, and she didn't want to get Dean in trouble.

"Were you close to him?" asked Nicole.

"Aha, you want to interrogate me now, huh? Guess I'll note your defensive nature in my article!" said Danielle.

"Hey, that's not fair! Just as you may be unfairly targeted in this, I am as well. And the police cleared my cafe," said Nicole. She was starting to lose her patience, and that happened very infrequently.

"Well, I don't mind telling you I am *thrilled* to finally get dibs on the juicy stories. F-I-N-A-L-L-Y! So expect to see me around a lot more often. And you can be certain I will be following up on *this* story," Danielle said quite confidently. She proceeded to head to the front door. Meanwhile, Nicole noticed Susie talking with a few stragglers from Knitting for Good in the back corner.

"By the way, I don't know what Dean sees in you anyway. P! H! D! Who cares!" she shouted, embarrassing Nicole in front of Susie and the few customers she had left. Nicole felt her face grow hot and couldn't wait to retreat to the back again, at least to catch her breath. Shaking from the stress, she thought about how she still couldn't overcome the criticism she faced since she earned her degree. Instead of people respecting her, they nearly made fun of her. It was a big "slap in the face" after she spent years of long nights and weekends taking classes, working on her research, and writing her dissertation, all while advancing her career full-time, not to mention all the difficulties she faced navigating the academic world of ego and politics to boot.

Feeling like a prisoner in her own establishment,

she finished packing her bag, left a note for Susie (who appeared to be doing damage control with the stragglers), and walked out the back door.

She never thought she'd be so excited to escape her own cafe as she did right then.

CHAPTER TWELVE

"Nicole! I didn't expect to see you darken my doorstep today. What a pleasant surprise!" remarked Gabriel, head of Information Technology (IT) at the University of New Jersey. A longtime friend and supporter of Nicole's, Gabriel was one of those more "seasoned" gentlemen who carried a certain air of wisdom about him, but not in a snobbish way. A kind and genuine soul, he had a way of sensing Nicole's concerns and worries throughout the years, particularly when it came to the tricky political issues at the university. He was perhaps the male equivalent to Nicole's dearly departed friend and original owner of the Cannoli Cafe, Bernadette, the one who entrusted Nicole to run the Cannoli Cafe upon her passing.

Nicole, still reeling from what had just transpired with Danielle Pruitt at her cafe, was quiet. She mustered a small smile and said, "Gabriel, I was hoping I could have a few minutes of your time."

Gabriel's office was very neatly organized—everything was in its place. He believed that organizing on the outside helped one to have more clarity on the inside. Perhaps that was one of the reasons he seemed so wise, Nicole often contemplated. Books were neatly placed on bookshelves along with family photos of beautiful children and grandchildren. Two empty chairs faced his desk, and he gestured toward one of the seats. "Please. Can I give you some tea?"

"No, thank you."

"I suppose this is about the article that just got published online? That reporter said your establishment should be renamed the Empty Cafe."

"It's up already? Oh dear—"

Gabriel waved his hands and interrupted Nicole. "So did you solve it yet?" He sipped his tea. Nicole thought she smelled peppermint.

"Solve what? The murder of Stuart Helm?" she asked.

Gabriel gave her "the look." Somehow he had a way of staring directly into her eyes as if to say, "Are you kidding me?"

"You'd better do it because that incompetent Detective Dawkins will look in all the wrong places."

"I'm sorry, can you repeat that?" said Nicole with a cocked head.

"I said you'd better solve it. Don't depend on that incompetent detective who will look in all the wrong places."

"Bingo, thank you, Gabriel! You just gave me an idea!"

Gabriel smiled. "Anything else I can help you with?"

"Yes, speaking of the detective—he still has my computer. I have some work I need to do for the department in the coming week—"

"He does? If I recall correctly, you have all your surveillance cameras tied into that computer, Nicole. That's not good, even if your cafe is empty right now."

Nicole flinched at his words. "Exactly. I was hoping you could suggest a temporary solution. I don't want to go out and buy an expensive computer —and I need one that can handle the computing power necessary for the surveillance system—but I don't know when this Detective Dawkins will finally give me back my original."

"Did you ask him?" said Gabriel.

"Not exactly. I've been getting my information second-hand through Dean when it comes to the police department. I heard he's upset I solved the last case so I've been trying to stay out of his way and not ruffle his feathers. I don't need any more trouble than what I'm already dealing with," said Nicole.

"You've learned how to pick your battles quite well, it seems. Guess my lessons counted for something." Gabriel chuckled.

"Of course you've been a huge help. I couldn't have survived this place without you!" Nicole gestured to the window which overlooked the beautifully landscaped campus green.

"As a matter of fact, I have a personal computer here that I was tinkering with. I was trying to set up better surveillance of my own office. But don't tell anyone. I have a feeling someone's been in here looking through my things, and I plan to catch them," he said in a whisper.

"Oh?"

"Here, take this computer. There is a webcam inside the computer, and I'm going to give you this second wireless webcam that will be tied into it."

"This would be perfect, Gabriel! To tell you the truth, I'm worried someone might try to plant something in my kitchen unnoticed while my surveillance system isn't working. I believe the killer knows computers well."

"Why do you say that?"

"Stuart Helm's computer was wiped out. They said the data is unrecoverable."

"Might be recoverable. I'd have to see it." Gabriel took another sip of his tea and placed his mug on the credenza behind him.

"I know, and I'm not sure how I could pull that off. But I've been thinking about it. Rosewood actually has a good cybersecurity division in the police department. They have to now with everything going on in the world. If they feel it's unrecoverable, it's safe to say that the killer knows enough to do some kind of damage again."

"Good point. Okay, well take this computer and webcam as I said. Do you think it would cover the kitchen and back door layout?" asked Gabriel as he opened the laptop between them on the desk.

"Yes, definitely. And I can set up the second webcam surreptitiously by the front counter, to look at the front door. But how does it work?"

"It's always running as long as you keep the computer on." Gabriel opened a program on the screen and pointed to it. "Here's the best part. You can set up the system to call your cell phone when it's activated to 'high alert' for a set period of time, say when you're closed. Here, I can set it up for you. What time does your cafe close tonight?"

"9, and Susie or I open it by 7 am."

"All set. You'll get a call on your cell phone when motion is detected, even in the dark. Then you can check the footage on the computer."

"Are you sure you don't need it right now?"

"Nah, I can catch my intruder next week," said Gabriel with a wink. "I'll sleep more easily knowing your situation is behind you. I have faith that you'll figure out who it is, and now you can at least leave your cafe with peace-of-mind. After all, you need more time for sleuthing." He smiled again, this time revealing practically all of his sparkling white teeth.

"Thank you, Gabriel," Nicole said gratefully. She appreciated that someone seemed to be in her corner, unlike Danielle Pruitt.

"I have to get to a meeting across campus, so I'd better let you go. Take care and be careful!"

"I will. Don't worry!" said Nicole, practically skipping out of his office.

CHAPTER THIRTEEN

On the way back to the Cannoli Cafe, Nicole drove mostly by way of local roads. She could have taken the highways back, but she avoided them so she could have more time to think about her conversation with Gabriel. She wanted to enter Rosewood feeling confident. Unfortunately, she left earlier in the day feeling like she should hide her face after being humiliated in her own cafe.

She thought about the case and tried to calmly review the facts, potential suspects, and how Detective Dawkins would look in the wrong direction. That was an important point Gabriel made, and the last murder case exposed his poor sleuthing skill—he hadn't interviewed the key people who might have led him to the murderer.

When Dean had updated Nicole and Lia at

dinner the night before, he mentioned how Detective Dawkins was focused on Danielle Pruitt. Nicole shook her head and said aloud, "Then it's not her. It must be Gornick or the Mongelli/Davison team." She saw that Gornick definitely wasn't a fan of hers, but she couldn't quite figure out how he would profit from her demise. After all, he was a numbers guy, being the business administrator and all. "Time to visit the Rosewood Coffee Shoppe!" she announced to her empty vehicle.

Feeling too jittery to manage parallel parking, she parked in one of the municipal lots about a block from the coffee shoppe. She rehearsed her planned interview with Bert and attempted to psych herself up to enter his establishment.

"Well, here goes!" she said to herself. She opened the door, immediately noticing how packed his shoppe was. Bert saw her from behind his front counter and waved for her to come forward.

"Well, hello there! Here, it's on the house! After all, I should be thanking you!"

Mortified, Nicole accepted the coffee cup Bert had just shoved in front of her. "Why should you thank me exactly?" she asked.

"Business, my dear, business! I don't care if your cafe did or didn't have anything to do with that reporter's death. All I know is that this place is *hopping* now!" Bert said, gloating. "Please, sit!"

Nicole looked across at him, a bit flustered. She sat down on a stool, realizing that if she came across friendly and willing to share in his excitement, she might eke out more information from him. "You do have a great shoppe, Bert. I'm glad that people are starting to realize that!"

"Geez, I guess Mongelli was right about you. You do have a nice personality. You should hate my guts right now!" said Bert.

Nicole took a sip of the coffee Bert had just poured her. *Market research*, she thought to herself. "Oh? I don't know a Mongelli." She thought to herself how a white lie wouldn't hurt anything. After all, it's not like she knew him personally. She only knew *of* him.

"Well, he knows you. He's an associate of mine. He was helping me do some research on the competition in this area. You know I serve cannolis now, too. I daresay mine are better! Just started serving them this morning, in fact!" Bert folded his arms across his chest, absolutely beaming.

Nicole's eyes widened. "Can't have enough cannolis in Rosewood, I suppose!" she said, stalling for time as she thought about his comment. "How would you know what mine taste like? I've never seen you in my cafe. Or did this Mr. Mongelli purchase them for you?"

Bert stiffened. "Vincent got them for me, yes. A few weeks ago, actually. Since then I perfected my recipe. In fact, I was about to send them to that Stuart Helm, but he died before I got the chance."

"Really?" Nicole asked, surprised.

"Well, of course! That jerk wrote such a stupid article on my shoppe! If you ask me, the world is a better place without him! I hated that guy!" Bert slammed a bunch of menus down that he had been organizing while talking with Nicole. "Mongelli and I decided we were done with that twit. It was time for him to go!" Bert said. He tapped his finger on the counter.

"Excuse me?"

Flustered, Bert said, "You know, we felt we were tired of his stupid articles. We thought there should be some more young blood in the paper. That article Danielle wrote about your cafe was excellent this morning. You should check it out online." Bert smiled devilishly.

"You know her?" Nicole was puzzled that he happened to mention not just Mongelli in the conversation, but Danielle too.

"You could say that. You know, I heard Dawkins was investigating her. I make it my business to know what's going on in this town." Bert tapped his index finger on the counter again, a habit he appeared to have when emphasizing a point. "Years ago, before you came back and before that dumb Stuart Helm also returned, I had a lot more business. Sure, people would go to Bernadette's cafe, God rest her soul. But the ones who wanted the real news came here, if you know what I mean."

Nicole was struggling in the conversation, feeling it was a bit over her head. She also worried if she was dealing with the mob directly or indirectly by speaking with Bert. And now he was talking about Bernadette?

She drank more of her coffee, hoping that her interest in his shoppe would get him to keep talking. "This is smooth, I like it." When she set her cup back down, she noticed a business card sticking out from under a pile of receipts. All she could see was part of the word; it looked like "—erminator." Her heart quickened. Did it perhaps say "Exterminator?" And could that really be a coincidence? Maybe he could have used a related poison?

Nicole decided to ask a few more questions and press her luck. "So, what can you tell me about Dawkins? I actually wondered if he could be a suspect. I know that sounds crazy." Nicole was testing him. While she was tossing and turning the night before, she had a fleeting thought that it *could* be Dawkins, but it wouldn't make sense if he really wanted to prove himself in this case. Yes, he could try to frame someone for the investigation, but wouldn't the police chief see through it?

"Well, if you want to think it's him, go right ahead. Wait till Mongelli hears this!" Bert let out a deep laugh.

"What does he have to do with it?" asked Nicole.

"In our experience, Dawkins is a pretty bad detective. Slips up a lot. He can think ahead, but not far enough at times. I don't think he could pull off a murder on his own."

"And how would you know exactly?"

"He spends more time driving around in his expensive cars than thinking about cases, I'll tell you that much. He used to come in here a lot. Trust me. I don't think he'll figure out who really murdered Stuart Helm. Whoever did it used a lot of strategy. After all, they framed you, killed Stuart Helm in the process, got Danielle promoted. And after all is said and done, Dawkins will get himself promoted, too!" Bert smiled, almost like a cheshire cat, before he went to the register to ring someone up.

When he returned, Danielle swallowed the rest of her coffee. "Well, this has been a very interesting conversation. I'd better go back to my cafe. Thank you for the coffee."

"Your empty cafe? Go right ahead. Thanks again for the business!" shouted Bert from across his shoppe as Nicole closed the door. She noticed everyone was staring at her.

CHAPTER FOURTEEN

"Why am I picking you up again? Is your car not working?" asked Lia.

Nicole closed the passenger door, placed her large tote bag on the floor, and buckled her seat belt. "Because Dean is busy on a job. And he probably wouldn't approve of my plan, anyway."

"What plan? Where am I driving to? What did you find out?" asked Lia excitedly.

"I'll explain on the way. 1500 Sycamore," said Nicole. "I'm baiting the killer tonight. At the university today, I got a special computer on loan from a good friend. If my theory is correct, someone who knows that my video surveillance is not currently working will plant the poison in my cafe tonight in an attempt to frame me. And my borrowed computer is going to capture it all on video!"

"What? Slow down. But first, what's at 1500 Sycamore?" asked Lia.

"Detective Dawkins' house," answered Nicole. "I spoke to Bert Davison today, and he made an interesting comment about Dawkins having expensive vehicles. I want to see what kind of property he has."

"He hasn't been a police detective that long, and I don't think they make that much money," said Lia. She arrived at a "Stop" sign and glanced over to Nicole.

"Exactly. I felt so confused after seeing Bert today. I actually left the coffee shoppe feeling like Vincent Mongelli, Bert, Danielle, and Detective Dawkins are all in on it! It's crazy!"

Lia pursed her lips and pulled the car over. "I can't drive and think. Explain this to me."

"Well, Bert Davison is definitely connected to Vincent Mongelli. In fact, he actually *bragged* to me about how Vincent bought cannolis from my cafe so that he could do research. But he lied about the timeline—he said he bought them weeks ago. Fortunately, we know from Dean that he bought them twenty-four hours before the crime."

"I don't see—"

"Here's my theory. Vincent Mongelli agrees to buy the cannolis so that he can poison Stuart, of course on Bert's behalf. Somehow they are also connected to

Danielle, because he seemed interested in seeing her promoted. And, he was unusually focused on Detective Dawkins being promoted, too, despite his association with Vincent Mongelli and the mob!" Nicole threw her hands in the air. "Why would the mob care about this detective's career? All this while Dawkins has expensive cars to drive around? Why is he a detective if he's so wealthy? It doesn't all add up!"

"Unless Dawkins has been keeping the police at bay, making sure they wouldn't investigate Mongelli and gang, and getting paid privately for it."

"Bingo! Can you go around the corner so we can see the house?" asked Nicole.

"Yes." Lia pulled her car back out on the road. As they swung around the corner, they entered a street full of mini-mansions.

"There it is! There it is! Oh no, there is Mongelli. I'm ducking!" Nicole bent down as much as she could, hoping he didn't see her. Lia kept driving.

"Where am I driving you to now?"

"Is it safe? To the cafe," answered Nicole.

"It's clear. He glanced over, not sure if he saw us." Lia shook her head. "I hope I'm not on their list now!"

"Hopefully not since it's dark out. You saw a few expensive cars and a gorgeous property, right?" asked Nicole.

"Definitely. Wow, I have to hand it to you, Nicole. You may be onto something." Lia's eyes widened. "I can't believe this. The police department is supposed to be protecting us. Instead, Detective Dawkins is protecting the mob! There is no reason Vincent Mongelli should be on the detective's property!"

"And that's exactly why Dawkins will be diverting attention away from *them*, by planting the poison in my cafe while my camera surveillance isn't working, since he knows he still has my computer!"

"Oh! And then try to say it was you all along! " said Lia. "But what would be your motive to kill Stuart in the first place?"

"I've been wracking my brain all afternoon about that, until I realized they wouldn't say I had a motive to kill Stuart. All they would need to do was focus on my incompetence in terms of running a cafe—that perhaps I mixed up something like rat poison with the rest of the ingredients, and that Stuart was simply an unlucky victim."

"You really think they would say you're incompetent?" asked Lia.

"Without a doubt. Besides, Dawkins still has all my old notebooks with my ingredient traceability and the rest is stored on my computer, still in his possession. I wouldn't be surprised if those notebooks or files magically disappear! We don't even know if he really registered them into evidence. How can we trust him?" Nicole scratched her head. She was finally slowing down. "You know, there was something about Bert Davison that reminded me of someone I dealt with years ago in the chemical industry."

"Really?"

"An individual from my past told my colleagues that I was incompetent. He was a good storyteller, kind of like a Bert. He would tell a story so believably, but he would leave out a few critical details, leading people to think I did something wrong. Trust me, it works, because people did start to believe I was incompetent back then, despite everything they knew about me. It took me a while to gain their trust again, even though I never did anything wrong."

"Why would someone do that?" said Lia, horrified.

"In that case, the individual didn't like that I got the job he wanted, and he did what he could to sabotage me. He also came across as one of those 'old boys' club' guys, you know? It didn't help that I was an intelligent woman." Thinking of those painful memories was difficult for Nicole; she felt her chest tighten again. "See, Bert has tons of customers now. Think about it. He can plant the seed to his crowd about my incompetence, while Dawkins plants the poison, and there you go. They get rid of Stuart, he gets a booming business, and I get carted off to jail."

Lia gasped. "Nicole, this is *not good*. What are you going to do?"

"When you drop me off, I'm going to set up this borrowed computer and webcam in my cafe. At closing time, I'll shut all the lights off. The back door doesn't lock easily, so I can leave it in such a way that it can be easily jimmied open."

"Pick you up at 9? By the back?"

"Yes. Maybe we can wait around the corner, and if my phone rings with the motion sensor alarm, I can return and check the computer footage. They won't know that it will be on, recording, the whole time they are inside."

"Let's hope it works. At least you shouldn't be in harm's way if it's just your computer monitoring the intruder." Lia pulled over so that Nicole could exit. Nicole smiled and gave her friend a big thumbs-up, a signal they shared over the years whenever they were about to achieve a milestone (and sometimes just to say goodbye).

CHAPTER FIFTEEN

When Nicole entered the Cannoli Cafe in the evening, she told Susie she could take the rest of the night off and that she would open up the next morning. While she trusted Susie a great deal, she didn't want anyone beyond Lia, who was essentially the "stakeout driver," to know what she had planned, in case it could put a wrinkle in the possible capture of Stuart Helm's murderer.

Ordinarily, it would have been difficult to spend time in her cubicle area in the evening, especially if Susie were out. Most nights were packed at the cafe. But this evening was quite different, no thanks to Danielle Pruitt. Instead of being disappointed, however, Nicole was actually grateful that the tide hadn't turned back quite yet; she needed the cafe to be empty so that she could execute her plan and set up the computer in time for closing.

After plugging in the computer, and planting the second webcam discreetly near the register, she opened up her phone to search the internet. It was 8:25 p.m. and she needed to kill time, but she didn't know what to search for first. She considered typing in combinations of the names of the various suspects and then decided not to, worried someone would walk in and catch her off-guard. Then she decided to see what was written in the obituary for Stuart Helm, wondering if it could yield any clues. She read it and didn't find anything that could help her detective work, but she did notice that Stuart's parents were still alive. *That's not how it's supposed to be; a parent should never have to bury a child*, she thought. Her eyes glistened, and she closed the browser on her phone.

She returned to the kitchen area, just to check the new computer-video setup one more time, when she suddenly heard a loud noise from out front and someone yelling, "Professor? Hello? Are you in here?" She shut the lights off to the kitchen and proceeded to walk to the front. Feeling uneasy, she grabbed a knife on the way to the front counter, just in case.

To Nicole's surprise, she saw a young man, perhaps college age, standing by the front door. "Can

I help you?" She discreetly put the knife on a shelf under the counter, out of view.

"Hi, I'm Gregory Gornick. Thomas Gornick's son."

Nicole was stunned. *What is he doing here?* she thought.

"I heard my dad was perhaps unkind to you. I'm sorry about that. In fact, he doesn't know I'm here. I was wondering if I could explain to you why I cheated on my exam."

Nicole felt a little alarmed. Maybe she was wrong. Maybe Thomas Gornick was out to get her, and he sent his son to the front of the cafe to distract her, while he was perhaps placing the poison in the kitchen area. *But the camera would catch that*, Nicole thought. But then she realized he may also try to kill her to make it look like suicide, so the footage wouldn't help, especially if he had the foresight to remove the computer. She started to panic. This was all happening before closing time and not according to plan.

"Why would you need to explain that to me, Gregory?"

"Because I really want to go to the University of New Jersey."

"You do?" asked Nicole, surprised.

"Yes, I want to be a mechanical engineer, and I

know they have a good program. The problem is, my dad wanted me to go to his prestigious university, and for me to major in business. He said his network would get me a job and that I'd make a lot of money." Gregory paused. "But honestly, I'd much rather build things. I love taking things apart and tinkering with them!" His face lit up as he described his interest in mechanical engineering. This was throwing Nicole off; he seemed sincere.

"I didn't realize that, Gregory. I wish I knew of your interest. Perhaps we could have talked earlier."

"I know I should have approached you sooner, but you know my dad can be a little...difficult."

"I don't really know your father," said Nicole. She glanced at her watch, a little nervous. 8:40. But she was also intrigued. Maybe she could get more clues from this conversation, or insight about Thomas Gornick, at least.

"He's never going support my decision." Gregory started pacing in front of the counter. "I don't care if I have to take out loans. That's how he controls me, with his money. But I'm sick of his expectations and want to live my own life," he declared. "Anyway, I'm here on a longshot. Can help me get into the university? I shouldn't have cheated on the exam, but I did it because of the pressure from my dad. Also, I'm not great at history, and that's the exam I cheated on. But I am great at chemistry, physics, and math."

"I'm not sure what admissions would say. You may have to enroll non-matriculated, prove yourself, and then be formally admitted. I might be able to set an appointment up with an admissions counselor I know to agree on a workable plan."

"Yes! Thank you!" Gregory had a huge smile on his face.

"Gregory, if you don't mind my asking. Why is your dad against public universities, or is it just the University of New Jersey?"

Gregory sighed. "He wants to preserve the way he grew up, in old money. But don't quote me on that."

"That's it?"

"Not exactly. On top of his self-preservation, he lost the love of his life to the University of New Jersey."

"Excuse me?" Nicole raised her eyebrows.

"A long time ago, Stuart Helm's father squandered the Taverson family's investments. They trusted Stuart's father, and he wound up bankrupting them. Eventually, Stuart's father got caught and he served some time; the Taverson family wasn't the only one affected by the scheme." Gregory shook his head. "You see, my dad was in love with Michelle Taverson in high school, and once her family went bankrupt, she had to go to the University of New Jersey on scholarships instead of following my father to his university. As time went on, she decided my father wasn't for her anymore. He was into the prestigious networks, and she enjoyed a life without them. She set out to prove herself so that she did not have to rely on her family for money. She did quite well and—"

Nicole, excited, raised her hands in the air. "Of course! Michelle Taverson is the Dean of the College of Engineering! She is extremely well-respected."

"Yes, and my father blames the Helm family for everything. He thinks if Michelle Taverson went to college with him, they would have married—"

"But your father moved on and married someone else. Doesn't he love your mother?"

Gregory's eyes teared up. "They coexist and put on a front, but he just married my mother because she was in the old money network. She is constantly trying to please him, and he is never happy."

"Oh my." Nicole was again starting to question her theory about the murderer. Unrequited love can drive people mad. Would Thomas Gornick go that far, to murder Stuart? And then she remembered the obituary—that Stuart's father was still alive, perhaps the true target depending on who the murderer was.

Did Thomas Gornick kill Stuart to get back at his father?

Nicole glanced at her watch. 8:57 p.m. "I'm sorry, Gregory. I need to close up. But thank you for visiting and sharing so much. Send me an email at the university with times you are available to come to campus and I will try to help you."

"Wow, you really are a nice professor lady. Thank you. And good night!" Gregory ran out of Nicole's cafe. She took the key from her pocket and locked the front door and then promptly turned out the lights. Now she was in total darkness except for the glow of the streetlight shining through the windows. She found the flashlight icon on her phone and pressed it. She needed to make her way to the kitchen and exit through the back door to meet Lia.

As she returned to the front counter, she thought she heard a noise. *It's in your head, Nicole*, she thought. She shuddered. And then she remembered to take the knife on her way back to the kitchen.

After she passed through the doorway, she scanned the kitchen with her flashlight. And then she saw the back of Detective Dawkins closing the door to her personal refrigerator.

He turned around and raised his gun.

CHAPTER SIXTEEN

Nicole gasped. Detective Dawkins stood before her, barely visible in her dark kitchen, pointing a gun at her. She decided not to make any sudden moves. She was still holding the knife in her right hand, discreetly kept to her side. Meanwhile, her left hand held her phone up, providing the little light that made Detective Dawkins visible.

Detective Dawkins spoke first. "I see you have that phone there. Don't even think about calling anyone or I'll shoot," he warned.

Nicole stayed motionless, her eyes fixated on the gun.

Dawkins laughed. "Scared, are ya?" He waved the gun a little in her direction. "You know, you never should have told Bert you solved the murder. He sent

Mongelli over with the news," said Detective Dawkins.

"What did you just place in my refrigerator?"

"Rat poison, but you probably knew that already, right? Did you see the exterminator card I left you at Bert's?"

Nicole was starting to panic. Was he baiting her the whole time? She now realized that Detective Dawkins would be the one to kill her yet make it seem like she killed herself. It would all be an illusion, a facade implying that her incompetence killed Stuart Helm. Further, she would be found dead with a gun in hand, obviously in despair over mixing rat poison with cafe ingredients.

What do you do when the detective, the one who is supposed to serve and protect, is the one who is the murderer?

She realized she should keep him talking as long as possible. She knew her phone would ring at 9 pm since the webcam alarm would kick in and sense the movement. But she wasn't sure if or how that could help her. Maybe he would think someone was looking for her? Or maybe that would prompt him then to kill her and run? And what about Lia? She would be waiting outside in her car. Would she realize something was wrong?

She decided she needed the call to be silent, to ensure she had as much time as possible to escape somehow. She didn't want to take the chance that the call might push him to kill her immediately.

"But Bert, Vincent, and Danielle are all in on it, right? You all participated in this plot?" she asked.

Dawkins moved closer to her, the gun shaking. "What's wrong with all you people? No one thinks I can handle a murder. Mongelli and Davison were laughing at the idea of me killing Stuart Helm. They didn't think I could pull it off! When I told them I did it, they didn't believe me!"

"I did give you full credit actually. It was Bert who said otherwise," said Nicole, hoping to cater to his ego a bit while she tried to press the volume button hard enough to bring her phone to silent.

"I decided to take matters into my own hands. I don't work for them anymore. I'm sick of their insults. And see? I did a great job, because you're the only one smart enough to figure out that I did kill that stupid reporter."

"Was that why you killed Stuart? Were you testing me?" asked Nicole.

"Yes, as a matter of fact I was. I wanted to show those guys I could pull off a murder without their help and get rid of the guy who ruined my credibility in the police force." Dawkins paused. "And I wanted to see how good you really are." He sneered. Then he stepped backward, moving closer to Nicole's refrigerator. "Too bad you didn't give me a chance to solve the last murder in town. Maybe Stuart would still be alive if you did. Well, shall I crown you before your death, for being so smart, Professor?"

"I don't understand. Why do you need to kill me? We can just keep this between us," pleaded Nicole. She was desperate. Then she saw her phone flicker for a second; she had a call coming in, most likely from the computer, but she didn't want him to think she placed it so she let it go.

"Huh, maybe you're not that smart. I need to kill you so that it looks like you're the murderer." Detective Dawkins kept the gun on Nicole while he opened the fridge and lifted a bottle. "See this rat poison? I'm leaving it right here." Nicole noticed he had leather gloves on once the refrigerator was open; the interior light helped illuminate him better.

"Next, I'll shoot you at very close range, and leave the gun in your hand after I sprinkle some gunpowder on you. They'll assume you felt hopeless—that you accidentally killed Stuart and then decided you needed to take your own life. I also planted a dead rat by the back door, just to complete the picture. Good, right?"

Nicole was shaking. She was wracking her brain, trying to figure out what to do. Since she was the one with the flashlight on her phone, she realized she had a certain degree of power. She could run, and she had the knife if he did catch her. Her biggest fear was that he could shoot blindly in the dark and possibly get her.

"Wow, you *have* thought of everything. Can I see the rat? I'll shine the light on it," she asked, nervously. This was the moment. Now, or never.

Detective Dawkins started pointing toward the back door. "Look, over there!" She quickly turned the flashlight off, threw the phone to unload it, and grabbed the key from her pocket while she ran to the front of the store. She kept the knife in her right hand in case he caught up.

She couldn't get to the door fast enough, though; she heard him catching up. When she reached the front area, she realized the glow of the streetlight was making her too visible, and that he'd be able to easily shoot her. She quickly hid under a stool on the other side of the counter, just a few feet from the front door.

She hoped and prayed someone might see what was transpiring through the window.

"Now, now, now. Why would you do that? I need

to shoot you at close range, you know that. Well, guess I need to get closer!"

Suddenly, he jumped on top of the counter and then jumped down, landing right on the other side, directly in front of her. She immediately jumped up, used her left hand to grab the hand with the gun, pushing it away from her with all her might while simultaneously trying to stab him with the right, but he was too strong; he was holding her right arm, practically breaking it. Nicole mustered all her strength and screamed, "Help!" At that very moment, she suddenly heard a crash through the front door. It was the police!

Chief Van Stone shouted, "Put your weapons down! Hands up!"

Dawkins looked around. He was completely surrounded. He let go of his grip on Nicole and put his gun on the floor; then he put his hands up. Nicole placed the knife on the floor and also raised her hands. Chief Van Stone made a motion with his head, and Dean popped up from behind, grabbed Nicole, and pulled her back. She was so relieved to see him. While he hugged her, she heard the chief say, "Dawkins, you have the right to remain silent..."

She pulled back from Dean and whispered, "How? How did you and the police know?"

Dean answered, "Your university friend—Gabriel.

Apparently the webcam was set up to not only call your phone, but his too. He was able to tap into the camera feed and saw you being held at gunpoint. He called 9-1-1."

Tears streaming down her face, she said, "Thank goodness. Gabriel turned out to be a true angel."

EPILOGUE

"Are we still on for Chez Juliette tonight?" asked Dean. He was dressed sharply in a black T-shirt and jeans for the Grand Reopening Party at the Cannoli Cafe. It was Saturday morning and the whole town seemed to be jammed inside.

"Definitely, Mr. Coogan. I could use a nice, quiet dinner and would love your company." She looked up and smiled at him.

"Nicole! Where's Nicole?" Despite all the noise in the cafe, Nicole could hear her aunt calling.

"Please, help her through!" she asked. Everyone parted to allow one of Rosewood's favorite residents, Lucia Capula, greet her niece. Nicole also walked forward to meet her.

"Oh! My dear niece!" Aunt Lucia grabbed Nicole, hugging and kissing her. "What were you thinking?

Please do not get involved in a murder investigation ever again!"

"I won't. Gunpoint twice in a row was a bit too much for me. I think I will leave it to the professionals from now on," Nicole answered. "However, I would say that the practice from the first murder helped me cope with the confrontation in my cafe the other night."

Lia approached them. "Nicole has a point. She could have been in there whenever Dawkins was going to plant the poison and it would have been bad timing."

Dean chimed in. "I was wondering why he didn't plant the poison the night before, when we were eating dinner at your house. Fortunately, Commissioner Van Stone had a stationed officer on premises until you re-opened Thursday morning. So his first opportunity was the very night you had set up Gabriel's computer."

"Well, I'm just glad you're safe now. Stick with Dean," said Aunt Lucia. "Dean, now don't let her out of your sight. I'm counting on you!"

Nicole, Dean and Lia all laughed. Dean and Lia both said, "Easier said than done!"

Suddenly, Nicole felt a tap on her shoulder. She turned around, and it was Vincent Mongelli. "Hello Nicole, I've never had the pleasure of meeting you personally, but I've heard all about you from your aunt." Vincent smiled at Lucia. She waved back. "Listen, I just want to apologize. Bert told me what you had said about Dawkins committing the murder. I went to his house to tie up some loose ends. You know, I'm trying to turn a new leaf, and Bert and I are working on some new, clean—I might add—business ventures. I told him what I heard and laughed. When he admitted to me that he did taint cannolis with rat poison and gave them to Stuart as a goodwill gift, I honestly didn't believe him so I didn't report it." Mongelli paused, looking down. "If I had reported it, you never would have been in harm's way. So, I'm very sorry." Nicole, Lia, Dean and Aunt Lucia all looked at each other, partially in shock. "Lucia, I'm sorry I didn't do a better job to protect your niece. As I said, I have big plans going forward, good plans. And Bert does, too. He also wishes you the best, Nicole. He's behind me somewhere and wants to speak with you."

All this attention and sincerity was making Nicole sentimental. "Thank you, I do appreciate your words." After she dabbed her eye, she happened to notice Danielle Pruitt furiously writing in her notebook while she was interviewing Don and Max a few feet away. She smiled, happy that her cafe would be reported as "not empty."

Lia whispered in Nicole's ear, "I heard she is getting a book deal. Depending on how successful the book launch is, she might quit the Rosewood Gazette! Apparently, she was buying cannolis from your cafe for inspiration. The title of the book is *Death by Cannoli*. Something about a priest who gets murdered by someone named Cannoli."

"Really?" asked Nicole, also whispering.

Bert suddenly came up from behind Mongelli and said, "Well, if I have to be in competition with someone, then I want it to be with you. I have to admit that I was hoping you'd move on from this town, especially when my shoppe tanked, but I think there may be room for both of us here in Rosewood after all. I'm glad you're okay and that Dawkins is behind bars now. He never should have killed Stuart Helm, that was going too far. And I'm sorry if I gave you the wrong impression."

Nicole grinned. "Thanks, Bert."

Bert suddenly grabbed a coffee mug and jumped on top of a table. He shouted, "To Dr. Nicole Capula! Hear, hear!" The whole cafe erupted in cheer, "Hear, hear!"

Nicole, tears streaming down her face, kissed Dean on the cheek and hugged Lia. She then squeezed and held her aunt's hands, grateful she was no longer holding that knife, fearing for her life. "I love you all so much. Thank you."

Dean replied, "And we love you, Nicole."

Lia stole a glance at her dear friend and gave her a big thumbs-up. Nicole returned her gesture with a glistening eye and the biggest smile Lia had ever seen.

RECIPES

These recipes are included for fun. Feel free to experiment with them. As always, please use caution and be mindful of kitchen/culinary safety practices!

Italian Baked Macaroni

Serves 6

Ingredients

    1 lb. ground beef

    1 lb macaroni pasta, cooked

    1 jar marinara/pasta sauce (or make your own—see second recipe below)

    ⅓ cup parmesan cheese (grated or shredded)

    1-½ cups shredded mozzarella

- Preheat oven to 375 deg F.
- Brown meat in a skillet. Drain the fat after browned.
- Spray a 13x9 baking dish. Spoon marinara sauce on bottom. Then layer in cooked macaroni, cheese, and ground beef. Leave the top with marinara and a mix of marinara sauce and remaining parmesan and mozzarella.
- Bake for at least 20 minutes (or heated through).

Easy Marinara/Pasta Tomato Gravy

Note: While I may be an engineer by training, I grew up watching my mother and grandmother make "tomato gravy" by heart. The tomato gravy is often cooked to taste in my family (there is no written recipe). I have provided an easy version which you can make very quickly (if you want the flavors to blend together longer, you can keep on low heat and stir often, or you can make it a day ahead and let it sit in the refrigerator and warm it up when you need it).

I often make this gravy on Sundays with macaroni (or spaghetti) along with meatballs on the side. It tastes even better the second day. I also make a large quantity of gravy so I can refrigerate it and use it at least three times for dinners throughout the week.

Ingredients

    2 cans crushed tomatoes (28 oz each)

    1 can tomato paste (6 oz)

    6 oz water (use empty tomato paste can)

    Garlic, crushed

    Red wine (optional)

Spices: basil, parsley, onion powder, italian seasoning, oregano, salt, pepper, red pepper (optional)

In a large pot, coat the bottom with olive oil. Let it warm up a little on medium heat and then put 1-2 teaspoons of crushed garlic in the oil. Then add the cans of crushed tomatoes, tomato paste and water. Stir often. Then add all the spices to taste. My mother's unscientific suggestion has always been: "Coat the top of the gravy with the spices." For me, this means some salt, lots of black pepper, lots of basil, parsley, onion powder, Italian seasoning and oregano, until there is an even layer of spices on top before I stir them in. I also like to add a few ounces of red wine. The smell of the gravy with the wine added will give your home that warm and cozy feeling, especially if you let it simmer on your stove on a Sunday afternoon!

You can use this gravy for many recipes, including the baked macaroni (above), lasagna, spaghetti and meat-balls, etc.!

Tip: For an even "fresher" taste, you can add an additional can of the peeled plum tomatoes and try to mash the tomatoes in the gravy! This will also stretch out the volume.

ICED COOKIE MURDER (CANNOLI CAFE MYSTERY SERIES BOOK 3)

This is the next title in the Cannoli Cafe Mystery Series (Book 3). It will be released on Christmas Day (Dec. 25, 2018) and is currently available for pre-order on Amazon.

Book Description

The most wonderful time of the year?

The residents of Rosewood have enjoyed a peaceful, murder-free fall season. Now that the holidays are approaching, everyone is excited for the upcoming Annual Christmas Cookie Competition. To the surprise and horror of the town, however, last year's cookie competition winner, Adam Tremblay, is suddenly murdered the day before the popular event.

As usual, amateur sleuth Nicole Capula is on the case with the support of her best friend, Lia, and her new beau (and private investigator), Dean. To complicate matters, Nicole's ex-fiance, Luke Gainsworth, unexpectedly shows up in town and quite coincidentally, as Nicole discovers Luke apparently knew the murder victim prior to his trip to Rosewood. Will Nicole be able to keep Dean and Luke from fighting over her long enough to solve the case (and sort out her feelings)?

This is the third book in the Cannoli Cafe Cozy Mystery Series by Lizzie Benton, set in a quaint town in New Jersey, in close proximity to New York City and its gorgeous skyline.

You may pre-order Iced Cookie Murder to receive it automatically on December 25, 2018!

ABOUT THE AUTHOR

Thank you for reading *Murder and Macaroni*! While the story and characters are fictional, a few elements of the story were inspired by my own life. For instance, like Nicole, my education was in the field of engineering. I also grew up and currently live in New Jersey, though Rosewood is certainly fictional. One last detail based on personal inspiration—my Italian-American grandparents' black labrador was named *Ringo*!

While the aforementioned elements are true of my own life, the entire story and all the characters are fictional, and any coincidences to any particular events or anything else are just that—coincidental and fictional.

I sincerely hope you enjoyed my second work of fiction, and if you'd like to be notified when my next book comes out, please visit:

http://lizziebenton.com

(I will only send an email when a future book is

published and available to read). Also, you are welcome to follow my Amazon Author page.

Thank you again for reading!

amazon.com/author/lizziebenton

ALSO BY LIZZIE BENTON

Cannoli Cafe Mystery Series

Murder and Macaroons

Murder and Macaroni

Iced Cookie Murder

Made in the USA
Monee, IL
22 February 2024

53938375R00080